Adrift!

Suddenly, unexpectedly, the floe shook and a loud crack shattered the stillness. Alika watched in horror as the dark expanse of water between the ice floe and the shore began to widen. *Three feet! Five feet! Seven feet!* Alika's body stiffened with fear and helplessness. The same thing had happened to several villagers without kayaks to reach the shore. Their floe had split off, and they were never seen again.

Alika didn't know how to swim, and even if his feet *were* to find bottom and he could wade across carrying Sulu...Even if they could reach land, they'd surely freeze onshore, turn into human icicles.

Going into the water would be a fatal mistake.

Ice Drift

Ice Drift

THEODORE TAYLOR

Harcourt, Inc.

Orlando   Austin   New York
San Diego   Toronto   London

www.HarcourtBooks.com

First Harcourt paperback edition 2006

Library of Congress Cataloging-in-Publication Data
Taylor, Theodore, 1921–
Ice drift/Theodore Taylor.
p. cm.
Summary: In 1863, two young Inuits, fourteen-year-old Alika and his
younger brother Sulu, must fend for themselves during the six months
they are stranded on an ice floe that is adrift in the Greenland Strait.
1. Inuit—Juvenile fiction. [1. Inuit—Fiction. 2. Eskimos—Fiction.
3. Brothers—Fiction. 4. Survival—Fiction. 5. Icebergs—Fiction.
6. Baffin Bay (North Atlantic Ocean)—History—19th century—Fiction.]
I. Title.
PZ7.T1286Ic 2006
[Fic]—dc22 2005055094
ISBN-13: 978-0-15-205081-8 ISBN-10: 0-15-205081-7
ISBN-13: 978-0-15-205550-9 pb ISBN-10: 0-15-205550-9 pb

Map created by Tracy Hargis
Text set in Spectrum
Designed by Lydia D'moch

C E G H F D

Printed in the United States of America

For editor Allyn Johnston,
who piloted this floe of words with great skill
—T. L. T.

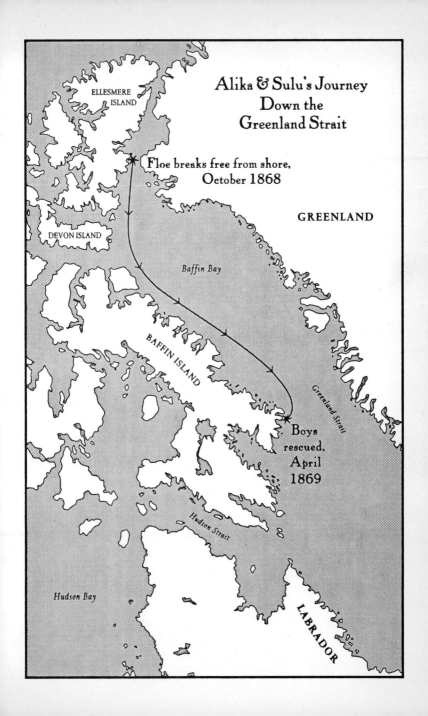

Alika & Sulu's Journey
Down the
Greenland Strait

ELLESMERE
ISLAND

Floe breaks free from shore,
October 1868

GREENLAND

DEVON ISLAND

Baffin Bay

BAFFIN ISLAND

Greenland Strait

Boys
rescued,
April
1869

Hudson Strait

Hudson Bay

LABRADOR

THE ARCTIC CIRCLE

The Arctic Circle, as laid down on maps, is a geographic
line of latitude drawn around the earth, parallel with
the equator and 23 degrees 30 minutes from the
North Pole. Within this circle lies the Arctic Ocean;
nearly all of Greenland; Spitzbergen, Nova Zemlya,
and other islands; northerly portions of Norway,
Sweden, Finland, Russia, Siberia, and upper Alaska
and Canada, including the new territory of Nunavut,
established in April 1999, with a population
eighty-five percent native Inuit. At the North Pole,
the sun rises and sets once a year; the moon, once a month.

THE HAYES ARCTIC EXPEDITION, 1860–61:
One incredible ice floe covered twenty-four square
miles. It rose twenty feet above the sea and reached
an estimated depth of 160 feet. The estimated
weight was six billion tons, a floating glacier,
expanding year by year, as the ancient ice, hundreds
of years old, remained frozen, fresh snow
accumulating and congealing into new ice above.

1

Alika, hand on his harpoon, his *unaaq,* ready for an instant kill, had been at the seal hole, the *aglus,* for three hours. His younger brother, Sulu, who had begged to join him on the hunt, napped beside him on the sledge. They were on the west edge of a large, thick ice floe attached to land in the Greenland Strait, waiting for a shiny seal head to appear. The floe was old. Perhaps it had broken off from North Greenland and had drifted across the narrow strait, refreezing against the remote Ellesmere Island bank.

The time was mid-October 1868, on the eve of the long winter darkness. The shallow noon light was already fading. Snow had fallen a week earlier and would stay until almost June. The caribou were mating, char were spawning, and the sea ice was forming. All over the Arctic, inhabitants, both human and animal, were preparing for the frozen siege.

Jamka, the lead sledge dog, had sniffed out the small hole where he expected a ringed seal would soon surface to breathe, and Alika had prepared for the day's hunt by building a windbreak of snow blocks and a snow-block seat next to the *aglus* that he covered with a square of polar bear hide to keep his bottom warm. An indicator rod of caribou bone was in the hole. When a seal came up, it might touch the thin rod, wiggling it and alerting him.

Many of Alika's elders often waited a day or two for just a single strike at the wily ringed seal or the bearded seal, the only two to spend the entire year above the Arctic Circle. But Alika didn't have the patience of his elders, and a worried glance at the snow-laden sky told him they should soon start for their village of Nunatak, which was seven miles south. A northwest gale was approaching. Alika could feel it coming, with its thick wind-driven snow. Winter weather was usually predictable eight hundred miles southwest of the North Pole. The stars had twinkled brightly the night before, often a sign of bad weather.

Descendants of the Thule people who had first

settled in the north a thousand years before, fourteen-year-old Alika and his brother, ten-year-old Sulu, were Inuit, meaning "mankind," and their diet was mostly from the sea, mostly cooked.

Alika said to Jamka, "You promised me a seal a long time ago."

The Greenland husky, dark eyes always seeming to have an intelligent expression, stared back as if to say, "But I didn't tell you when."

Alika sighed.

Jamka squatted near Alika. At 110 pounds, he was a huge dog, with black-and-brown fur six inches thick. His undercoat was naturally oily to prevent moisture from reaching his skin. His bushy tail curled over his back. His ears were small, like those of most other Arctic animals, offering less area to absorb the cold of forty-five degrees below zero. He had a broad chest and big bones. There was wolf blood in him. In the Inuit tradition, the village children trained their dogs for sledge work. Alika had trained Jamka.

When Alika was seven years old, he and Jamka had bonded in an emergency, and they had been almost inseparable ever since. One September day, when the ice was still thin on a lake two miles from

Nunatak, Alika was fishing for char when the crust broke. Into the water he went. Jamka pulled him out by the parka hood and dragged him home. Alika well remembered looking up at Jamka's wet belly as he slid on his back along the snow. He was convinced that Jamka thought like a human, and he trusted the dog with his life.

He looked over at Jamka and said, "I hope your nose isn't drying up." The adult hunters trained the dogs to sniff the seal breathers. Papa Kussu had done that.

Jamka continued to stare at the hole.

Ringed seals usually surfaced to breathe in what the white man judged as every seven minutes, but it was possible for them to stay down as long as twenty.

There were hundreds of the cylinder-like holes dug from beneath the ice. Three-hour waits were nothing, because the hunter could never tell which holes were being used. Only dogs like Jamka had that talent, and even they were often wrong.

Alika rose and called to the other dogs that were half buried in the snow. It was past time to go home.

Jamka stood up, also looking at the quickly darkening, threatening sky. Very experienced, Jamka seemed to sense danger in guiding the team, as if he knew exactly where hidden crevasses were; where the thin ice was. He'd fought polar bears and been wounded by them. He was the best lead dog Kussu had ever owned.

Then suddenly, unexpectedly, the floe shook and a loud crack shattered the stillness. Alika watched in horror as the dark expanse of water between the ice floe and the shore began to widen. *Three feet! Five feet! Seven feet!* Alika's body stiffened with fear and helplessness. The same thing had happened to several villagers without kayaks to reach shore. Their floe had split off, and they were never seen again.

Alika didn't know how to swim, and even if his feet *were* to find bottom and he could wade across carrying Sulu, water would seep into his polar bear pants and sealskin boots and underpants. Even if they could reach land, they'd surely freeze onshore, turn into human icicles. He needed time to cut snow blocks, build a small house, and start a seal-oil fire to dry their clothes. Going into the water would be a fatal mistake. The cold would kill them.

As he watched the shoreline fall away, Alika guessed that an iceberg aimlessly sailing slowly south down the strait, a ghostly and deadly mountain of ice, had rammed the floe, tearing it away from the permafrost shore, the always frozen earth. Now they were trapped in the gloom on a ship of ice, surrounded by hundreds of smaller ice cakes. The distance from shore would surely widen. Maybe they'd lose sight of the white-encrusted land completely. Total afternoon darkness was also near. They might not even see the village, where they lived with Papa Kussu and Mama Maja, as they slowly passed it. Unless they were very close, shouting would do no good in the wind and night.

Sulu had awakened, his small face a ball of terror. Alika said, "Don't worry, Little One, the wind will blow us back to shore." But he knew that chance was indeed slim. The prevailing wind this day was from the west, opposite of what they needed to reach shore again. He spoke in Inuktitut, the native language.

Thinking mostly of the Little One, Papa's name for Sulu, Alika shook the fear out of his head and tight stomach. One member of their village, old Miak, had survived being trapped on a big drifting floe. His terrible passage had taken months before he was rescued hundreds of miles down the strait by hunters. Alika tried to remember what Miak had said: "Get rid of the dogs. You'll be lucky to feed yourself. Toss them overboard. They'll run for home and alert the village. Build yourself an *iglu*. Watch out for bears. Don't go outside unless you have a rifle..."

Shore at this point was still only fourteen or fifteen feet away from their floe. Alika quickly unharnessed all the dogs except Jamka and pushed them into the water. *Nanuks,* polar bears, were always hungry, and Jamka would be the best defense against them. He knew their strong odor.

The six dogs paddled ashore, and Alika watched as they climbed up onto the bank and shook the water from their tough coats. They moved out into the closing dusk as a pack. Ideally, they'd run straight to the village, *unless* they encountered a bear. They'd surely attack it, Alika knew, and all six could be killed. He hoped the *inuas,* the always watching and listening heavenly spirits, would direct the dogs away from any prowling *nanuks.*

Alika thought that if the dogs arrived safely, his papa and the other villagers would quickly figure out what might have happened. *Only Alika could have unharnessed the dogs! He must be injured or, worst of all, adrift on a floe with no way to reach shore. Sulu has been missing all day and is undoubtedly with Alika. Poor Little One.*

Alika put his arms around his brother and said, "Don't be afraid. Papa has put everything on the sledge that we'll need. Once the dogs reach home, Papa and the other men will launch the big boat and paddle out to find us. We'll build a small house. We'll stay here near the *aglus* and hunt after we build the house, all right?"

Sulu nodded. He was almost too frightened to speak but did manage to say, "We can't use the sledge. The dogs are gone."

"We can use parts of the sledge, and everything that's on it," Alika said. "You'll see."

"What happened, Alika?"

"An iceberg hit the floe and broke it from shore."

"Why did the berg hit us?"

"Bergs have no brains, Little One."

Like Alika's, Sulu's intense eyes were black; his hair, straight and black, too. His caribou-fur parka hood framed a reddish-brown face that was holding back tears.

Rather frail and sometimes sickly, Sulu was an apprentice to the old ex-hunter Etukak, and his soapstone carvings of birds, a most difficult subject, were already the talk of Nunatak. Etukak said young Sulu was very talented.

Everyone in the village knew that Sulu was different and remarked about it. Mama called him "the gentle one." And he had that strange love of birds. He'd never put an arrow through a dovekie or an owl or a raven. And in the summer hunts, if he found a bird with a broken wing, he'd try to fix it.

Alika had seen him turn away when a seal was killed; when a caribou or musk ox was brought down; even when one of the thousands of hares was trapped and killed by Mama.

Out of Sulu's hearing, his papa and mama had talked about him—Papa dismayed that he might not hunt, his mama understanding. Alika had overheard them several times.

Suddenly the storm raged in from the west, with roaring wind gusts driving the snow. Alika turned the sledge over and gathered Sulu and Jamka behind it. These western storms were usually short-lived, and the boys had no choice except to huddle together and wait for it to pass. Alika shielded Sulu with his body. Storms were routine for Jamka. He just went to sleep.

Alika thought of home and the safety of their village, which was located fifteen miles from the west coast of Greenland across the strait. They could walk or sledge to Greenland on solid ice during the winter. Nunatak was the most modern settlement in the High Arctic, because of the nearby wreck of the American ship *Reliance*, a three-masted sail-and-steam vessel. Wooden hulled, it had been crushed by floe ice ten years earlier.

When its crew of fifty-five men, plus sixty dogs, abandoned the *Reliance*, the villagers stripped its hull inside and out, even to the ship's brass bell. Only the steam engine was left to rust away. The *Reliance*, a fine new ship, had been headed for the Arctic Ocean, with plans to send four sledges, the captain, and sixteen crewmen to the North Pole. They would have been the first humans to reach that celebrated geographic goal. But the *kabloonas*, the white men, had no idea of the power of huge slabs of ice and the tides.

Although it was home to some of the animals he needed to hunt, Kussu and the other villagers had always feared the ice. Alika did as well. It could crush anything in its way. With wind and currents pushing it, with its rumbling, screeching, thundering, or sawing noises, it could send towers of frozen water into the air and create vast ice landscapes of sharp hummocks, or hills. The *Reliance* had offered little resistance.

Alika went with his papa to the explorers' ship before and after it was crushed, amazed at what he saw; amazed at how the white men lived aboard that three-masted giant *umiak,* with its steam engine. It burned something called coal. The men gave him fancy food that made him throw up. What they clearly did not understand was ice. They were helpless when the hull popped open like the full stomach of a musk ox. Earlier they'd shown the villagers the huge timber ribs of the ship, saying they were unbreakable. The villagers had laughed and laughed. The *tuvaq,* the sea ice, could destroy anything.

After the crew and the three Inuit dog handlers left on sledges for the few settlements en route to Canada's Hudson Bay, far to the south, the residents of Nunatak put every inch of wood on their sledges as well as every single pot, pan, sheet, blanket, every item of left-behind food, and every lump of coal. They made trip after trip back to the village for a whole summer. Alika had helped.

And so what had been one-room sod-stone-and-sealskin dwellings were now made of wood, with roofs and wooden doors and wooden floors. There was even a proud community hall building, courtesy of the *Reliance* wood.

Nunatak then became remarkable and exceptional because the few coastal settlements from Ellesmere on down to Baffin Island and the Hudson Strait were really just summer tented and winter *iglu* hunting camps. Unlike Nunatak, those camps were not meant to be permanent. Nunatak, once a collection of temporary makeshift huts and *iglus,* could now properly be called a village.

From the ice rises steam fog, sea smoke, frost smoke, silence, or angry noise. The Inuit had to live with the ice and sometimes die on it.

2

The six sledge dogs, Nattiq in the lead, arrived in the late night at the snowbound village. The dogs often fought one another if not harnessed, mainly over food, but they seemed to sense the urgency of this event. Fortunately, they had not encountered a bear since leaving Alika and Sulu.

In the wind and swirling snow, they howled loudly outside Kussu and Maja's timber-and-sod dwelling. Kussu opened the door within seconds and went out, shocked to see the team without the sledge and his sons. As if the dogs might answer, Kussu yelled at them, "Where are the boys? Where is Jamka? Where are they? Tell me!" Kussu and Maja had been worrying since late afternoon. Sulu was always around the village; not this time.

Ice sparkled on the dogs' coats and hung down from their underbellies. Maja cried out, "They've been in the water. Look!" Snow pelting her smooth brown face, she yelled again, over the wind, "Could Alika and Sulu be adrift?" There was always that dreaded possibility when the villagers were seal hunting on the floe ice, but it happened rarely.

"Maybe!" Kussu yelled back, face taut with fright.

"We must go after them!"

"Of course!" Kussu shouted. "Of course!"

He ran to the village bell from the *Reliance* and began to ring it. Their sons were in danger. The boys might die.

Maja yelled at the dogs, "Why did you leave them?"

Inside again, Maja asked, "What happens if Alika is hurt? Sulu doesn't know enough to help."

"Sulu probably knows more than you think," Kussu answered. "He's hunted with us. He's seen *us* get hurt."

"If only the other men were here, we could have a search party, go out with all the dogs and sledges," Maja said. There were more than 150 dogs in the village. "The young women could go, too."

All the men of the village, except for the shaman Inu, the spiritual leader, and two feeble male elders, had gone inland to kill caribou and musk oxen for meat and skins. Each family needed thirty full skins every year to make clothing. It was a must, the final land-animal hunt before the long darkness. Kussu had planned to join them in the morning, after Alika returned with the sledge.

"Wishful thinking," said Kussu. "We have only our team. We have to make a decision, Maja: Go out alone with the dogs or try to find the floe from kayaks and hope they're on it."

Maja shook her head. "You decide."

Kussu thought a moment. "Let's find the floe."

Knowing the chances of finding their sons were slim if they were on a floe, Kussu said, "We'll look for them as soon as the storm blows over." Rescue attempts would depend solely on Kussu and Maja. Inu was too old to help, as were carver Etukak and Miak.

Maja nodded. She was a strong woman, with high cheekbones, penetrating eyes, and powerful hands. She was almost as good as Kussu at hunting and trapping out on the tundra or paddling a kayak—and just as brave.

Kussu soon went back outside and placed the dogs in their shelter. He fed them and then checked the kayaks, which had not been used since summer.

Maja quickly prepared dried fish from the summer hunt and they ate. In some respects, they were twinlike in size and appearance, except Kussu had a thick black mustache and goatee.

Kussu said, "If Alika went where I told him to go, the floe will pass here. But with luck the wind will drive it toward Greenland." There might be safety in Greenland. There were more villages over there.

"Why did you send Alika to the ice?" Maja asked, suddenly angry. "Winter is almost here."

"To hunt seals, of course. He's a man."

"He's still a boy. And why didn't you check the sledge to see if Sulu was on it?" Maja continually worried about Sulu's health.

"I was too busy talking to Niuinia about going out for caribou tomorrow to even think of Sulu."

Maja let out a disgusted breath.

They both knew that the size and depth of the floes controlled the speed of drift. The depth in the middle of the floe could be ten or fifteen feet or more, like a keel, but it would be thinner along the edges where it had been attached to land. The floe might run aground. They could hope for that. It had happened before.

After the three darkest months, the white man's November, December, and January, hunters sometimes went out on the moving ice for seals to feed their families. They'd even set up camps on the floes, going back to the mainland by kayak. But there was no guarantee this would happen. Kussu knew there could not be a worse time for his sons to be on the ice, if that's where they were, due to extreme cold and often thick darkness.

In the early hours of the new day, the gale died out as suddenly as it had begun, and Kussu and Maja dressed in their sealskin jackets with drawstrings at the hoods and wrists. The jackets also cinched at the waists, where they attached to the kayaks. Inuit inventions, the light ocean kayaks were made of wooden frames and covered with sealskin. Hunters sometimes attacked walrus or whales in them, two kayaks tied together, and sometimes they disappeared in their frail boats, blown out to hostile seas. Kussu and Maja knew that it was into this heaving theater of ice that Alika and Sulu may have gone.

Finally, Kussu and Maja lifted their kayaks and

carried them several hundred yards to the shore. Chunks of pancake ice mingled with the dark waters in no pattern. The winter freeze, thick enough to carry the weight of man or animal but not enough to stop a moving floe, would soon set in.

Without speaking, they launched the boats and slid into them, fastening themselves into the cockpits. Each kayak was twenty feet long, nineteen inches wide, and ten inches deep. If Kussu and Maja were lucky enough to locate the floe, they'd insert Sulu and Jamka into the covered bow of one boat and Alika into the other one, snug as fingers in gloves.

As the storm clouds vanished to the east over Greenland's mountains and the gale wind became a cold breeze, the waxing moon lit up the slivers of the kayaks. The water was calm again but littered with glittering pieces of ice. There was only one human sound, the rhythmic slosh of their paddles. Inside the cockpits, Maja and Kussu were already beginning to sweat, despite the subzero temperature. They guided around the chunks of frozen pack ice.

The sky was impaled with stars. Some Inuit believed that the stars were holes in the sky created by the passage of dead bears into the eternal light.

Kussu and Maja knew the Big Dipper as a herd of reindeer; the Pleiades as a dog team in pursuit of a bear; the belt of Orion was a cut by an Inuit into a steep snowbank to enable him to climb to the top. But they did not navigate by the stars this night. They paddled straight east. They could see Greenland's mountains in the distance.

Frost smoke set in during the first hour, coming up like fog. Kussu shouted across to Maja, "We must keep going!..."

She shouted back her agreement.

Four hours later, they still had not sighted the suspected floe in the brilliant moonlight. The muscles in their arms could no longer guide the kayaks away from the random ice impacts. The current had carried them south, but they finally made it safely back to shore, perhaps six miles downstream. They were exhausted.

Like most hunters, they knew what to do. They crawled down into their kayaks, pulling the sealskin aprons over the cockpits, and sadly went to sleep.

Kussu awakened after about six hours, relieved himself, and tapped on Maja's kayak. She soon pushed her cockpit cover open with one foot, crawled out saying "I'm hungry," and stretched.

"So am I," said Kussu. They hadn't brought any food along.

Looking out at the sea was useless, but Maja shouted, "Alika! Sulu!"

Defeated, Kussu said, "Let's go."

They began walking north, carrying their kayaks on their shoulders. They had to cross several creeks and inlets, and one river, hoping the ice had frozen enough to bear their weight. If it cracked, they would do what all kayakers did—put their boats down and slide them with their mitts until the ice was safe.

They reached Nunatak about noon and reported to the anxious women who greeted them that they had failed to find their sons. The floe might have already passed the village, or it might have grounded up to the north, not close enough for the boys to walk ashore.

Kussu said tiredly, "We must trust Alika to bring both of them back here safely." His face was grave. Maja's was as well. She lived for her sons.

There were solemn nods from all those encircling the parents. But everyone knew Alika was only fourteen, and Sulu only ten. They also knew the weather and the ice were heartless and unforgiving, and the season of darkness could be so cold that even the wolves would stop hunting.

Old Miak said, "I'm sure Alika built an *iglu* to stay in last night."

Kussu agreed. "He is a smart boy."

The shaman Inu had come out of his house, the big raven Punna on his shoulder. He said, "I will send a message to them."

The villagers nodded.

Maja and Kussu then borrowed a sledge and hooked their dog team to it to search the coast to the north in hopes that the floe had hung up there. Their kayaks were on the sledge, as well as a skin bag of dried char.

Both of them had traveled north before while hunting, and they took the same general route near the shore, exchanging places riding the sledge and running behind it every several miles. The moonlight reflected down, white as caribou milk.

Nattiq and the other dogs, happy to be on the trail, were performing well, and the alabaster of the land provided enough illumination so they could see any snow-covered rocks. Nattiq was likely to steer around them, anyway.

Finally, they reached the area where Alika had probably hunted. There was no sign of their sons. But there was a scar of ice on the bank where the floe had been. In the dimness, it stretched out of sight. Their sons were adrift in the Greenland Strait, without doubt.

Kussu said, "That floe must be four or five miles long." He wrapped his arms around Maja, who was silently weeping. They slowly began their return journey to Nunatak, sitting on the sledge together.

En route, Kussu studied the Milky Way—that faintly luminous band, stretching across the heavens, composed of innumerable stars too distant to be seen clearly—as if an answer might be found there. The Milky Way was the track made by the Raven's snowshoes. According to the Inuit, the Raven had created Earth.

The largest bergs usually broke off from the Greenland glaciers, drifting south or east in the currents, some flowing along the Canadian shore. Some then traveled into the North Atlantic Ocean and sank ships. Usually, only roosting birds were passengers.

3

The night sky had cleared as the clouds advanced toward Greenland, and the floe moved steadily south, under the moonlight.

The moon, Tatkret, was male, and the sun, Sikrinaktok, was female. Brother Moon was now providing bright light, and Alika thanked him for it.

Alika and Sulu and Jamka, half buried in snow, had emerged from behind the sledge to dust themselves off and start building a small, domed *iglu* for temporary shelter. It would be about five feet high. First, the boys looked back at the glassy, shining berg that had launched them. Alika guessed it was fifty feet high.

He said, "We'll go back there in the morning. We have work to do now."

The Little One nodded. Jamka sat down to carry out his role as bear guardian. The *nanuks* were around day and night, fair weather or foul.

Sulu said, looking over toward the shore, "Brother, how close will we come to home?"

"I don't know," Alika answered. "The gale blew us out. I don't know how fast we're traveling." They might have already passed their home, he thought.

Alika and Sulu were fortunate that Kussu always made certain the hunting sledge, with its wooden runners and caribou-antler braces, was fully equipped for any emergency. In addition to the *Reliance* rifle and ammunition reserved for bears and inland hunting, there were *Reliance* steel knives strapped to the frame, each for a special purpose. There was a bow and arrow, which made it possible to save bullets for the bears and an extra harpoon. There was also a *Reliance* stove vessel used to burn seal oil for drying wet clothing, heating, and cooking.

Kussu had also stocked the sledge with fifteen pounds of frozen seal meat and ten pounds of dried char, sealskins, an extra parka, caribou mattresses and sleeping bags, a sealskin rope, and a half dozen other survival items. He had selected carefully, well aware that in addition to his own life, the lives of Maja and their sons might depend on what was carried on the sledge.

As Alika unstrapped the knives, Sulu said, "We should have brought a kayak so we could just paddle ashore."

"We should have stayed ashore." Alika sighed, a touch of annoyance in his voice.

"Look, we'll get out of this, believe me. It may not be tomorrow or even next week, but we'll find a way, I promise," Alika said.

"How?" Sulu asked.

Alika sighed again. "At this moment, I don't know, but we'll find a way."

Sulu was quiet for a moment, then asked, "Could the sledge float?"

Alika sighed yet again. "Not with us on it. Let's go to work."

He pulled out a square of sealskin to use as a broom to sweep away the new snow and expose the hardpack beneath. For years while on hunts, Alika had been helping his father build temporary houses. He'd also built a number by himself. It was simple: Cut the building blocks out of hard-packed snow and place them. But finding good packed snow was not all that easy. If his harpoon shaft went down into it smoothly, the snow was apt to be usable. And Sulu was strong enough to help carry the cut blocks.

In less than three hours, they completed the small *iglu*. Then Alika laid down insulating floor skins while Sulu brought the caribou mattresses and sleeping bags in. Jamka was already inside and would share his body heat when the brothers stretched out on either side of him.

Sulu said, "I wish I hadn't come with you yesterday."

"I wish the same thing," Alika replied truthfully.

"I didn't tell Mama I was coming."

"You told me you did."

"I didn't know this would happen."

"Neither did I," Alika said sharply.

Sulu tried very hard to keep tears from rolling down his cheeks, and Alika saw his chin quiver. Alika stepped over and hugged his little brother. "I didn't mean to make you cry," he said. What else could he do but hug him and listen to what he said? Make them a team.

———

Alika started a fire by lighting the seal oil Kussu had stored on the sledge in a walrus intestine. He used a bow drill held between his teeth, and rotated the rod by swirling it with sealskin rope to make a spark in a small notched piece of board from the *Reliance.* The wick was dried moss. At home he used an iron pyrite to make the spark.

Alika left his papa's rifle just outside the *iglu* to prevent heat condensation from collecting in the barrel, causing rust. Alika had fired it several practice times a few years back.

Sulu said, "It's cold in here."

Alika had to suppress a laugh. It was cold everywhere. His brother hadn't slept in an *iglu* very often. Maybe a dozen times when out hunting with the family.

Alika said, "It'll warm up soon."

The final act of the night, before putting out the fire and bedding down in their sleeping bags, was eating a supper of wafer-thin frozen raw seal meat. Jamka, on his belly, chewed and grinded away loudly on his piece, his canines long accustomed to such meals. Alika and Sulu had to suck the frozen meat before it was soft enough to chew on. At home Mama would always boil the evening meal over

their oblong platterlike *qulliq,* the combined lamp
and stove that provided both light and heat and was
also used to dry clothing.

Sulu and Jamka soon went to sleep, but Alika lay
awake a long time, worrying and wondering about
the size of their floe. How long was it? How wide? A
day's walk to the end? How far would it travel until
it began to break up into pack ice? What else was living on it? Certainly bears and the white arctic foxes
that closely followed the bears to eat seal remains.
No humans likely, although Greenlanders might
have come out to hunt seals. But they'd quickly go
back to their settlements in their boats once the floe
began to drift south.

The only real enemy they might face out on the
floe was the polar bear. Alika wasn't certain he'd be
able to kill a bear with his first shot. If he missed while
Jamka was battling it, which was bound to happen, he
might not have time to reload. He was worried about
that. Jamka was not really a match for a fully grown
nanuk. It would take three or four dogs to bring a bear
down. Not even Jamka was that powerful.

Alika heard Sulu's muffled voice. His brother
had awakened.

"Will we be back in time for the feast?" Sulu asked.

"I'm sure we will," Alika said. Maybe Sulu had been dreaming? Such a strange question in the middle of the night. Maybe he was hungry?

The feast was the weekly *alupajaq* in the community hall. The men gathered around a seal and cut it up. They told hunting stories. The women came together to listen and talk about the seal and about how fortunate they were to eat well. The best parts of the seal were presented to the women and children. It was a happy time for all. Alika thought that many weeks might pass before they'd attend another *alupajaq*.

What they needed badly was a strong gale from the northeast that would jam the floe against the western shore, enabling Alika, Sulu, and Jamka to jump off onto the land. But unfortunately, there weren't often gales from the east this time of year.

"I was dreaming about *aalu*," Sulu said.

Alika moved over on the sleeping platform to comfort his brother. "After we get a seal, I'll make you *aalu*," Alika said. *Make sure the meat is very lean and clean; cut it into tiny pieces and put them into a bowl, adding a few drops of melted blubber, a few drops of seal blood, and a little ptarmigan intestine, and stir briskly with your fingers.* The sauce was delicious when smeared on seal. "I promise I'll make *aalu* if we can find a ptarmigan." Anything to take Sulu's mind off being adrift, Alika thought.

Sulu said soberly, "Use something else besides bird intestines." There was Sulu's bird obsession again.

"I'll try," said Alika, not having the faintest idea of what to substitute.

But his mind wasn't really occupied with fixing a treat for his brother. Soon the darkness would descend and last at least three months, including many days and nights when the weather would force them to stay inside—force them to give up hunting. Bad things could happen. Starvation, sickness, even *piblikoto,* craziness. Within Alika's memory, one woman had committed suicide during the long polar night.

Before drifting off to uneasy sleep, Alika decided on the next day's schedule. As early as possible, they would get settled by a seal hole. Food was the priority. *Food is always a priority.* Exploring and building a larger house could come later. Miak had been right. They must prepare for a long stay.

Round-faced, puffy-eyed Miak had spent almost six months on his drifting floe before being rescued. *Six months!* Alika couldn't bring himself to think that would happen again. The good spirits wouldn't allow it, he thought.

Surfaces of the huge floes were seldom smooth. The howling winds made cuts and crevices. At work beneath the floes crosscurrents pushed upward, forming ridges, the hummocks, sometimes thirty feet high.

4

Alika awakened slowly in the morning, again thinking about where they were and what had to be done for survival; then he crawled out the *iglu* entryway to relieve himself. Jamka followed him. Sulu still slept. The small shelter had served them well overnight. They'd slept warmly. In fact, they were warmer out here on the ice than they would have been on land, above the permanently frozen ground.

They were well equipped for the frigid weather. Their parkas of caribou hides, one inner suit with fur next to their bodies and an outer suit with fur outside, were light and airy and extremely warm; then bear trousers, sealskin underpants, and fur-lined mitts; their socks were made of hare fur.

The sky was dim and gray, casting dark shadows over the floe hummocks and western mountains as well as those to the east in the Greenland distance. Aside from the murmur of the water as their ice ship sailed slowly on, there were no sounds. No wind was blowing, a condition that wouldn't last, Alika knew. Though his body was warm, he shivered from the invading loneliness and thoughts of the arrival of nearly total darkness.

There were only a few days left before the sun would sink below the horizon and not rise again for three whole months. Could they survive it? Old Miak had done so, of course, facing starvation at one point. But then, Miak had had a lifetime of experience beforehand, a lifetime of winters, and was a seasoned hunter.

Sulu soon crawled out of the tunnel. He asked, "Will Papa come out and rescue us today?"

"Let's hope so," Alika replied, "but meanwhile, we have to build the larger house just in case he doesn't come out for a few days. If a blizzard begins, we'll just stay inside and play games."

Sulu nodded. He knew all about blizzards. The wind could blow him off his feet, tumble him carelessly like a ptarmigan feather. He rubbed Jamka's muzzle.

Alika added, "We need freshwater. Remind me." There were a few frozen pools of freshwater from the scant summer rains on the floe. They were easy to spot. He'd use an ax from the *Reliance* to dig out a chunk and melt it. They could also eat snow to quench their thirst in an emergency.

Alika already knew the sledge, with its survival treasures, would eventually be lost as the floe broke up. Far to the south, they would lose their house, too. But he decided not to discuss that with Sulu. Later in the day, he'd strip the sledge and store everything in the small *iglu* to make more space in the larger one.

He said to Sulu, "Let's start the big house, then we'll eat, then hunt."

"I'm very hungry," Sulu said. For one so thin, he was always hungry.

Alika answered, "Suck on some seal meat or char, and feed Jamka while I cut blocks."

This time they'd start by building a knee-high sleeping and cooking platform out of the snow blocks as their papa had always done. The round ceiling would be higher than Alika's head. The floor would be eighteen inches below the outside surface to avoid the wind. But Alika would use the same method as the night before, quickly cutting the blocks with the snow knife. He'd start an inner-leaning spiral until the domed structure was completed, with a windbreak outside the tunnel to help keep out frigid air. Both Inuit and Eskimos had been doing this for centuries.

For a while, Jamka watched as the boys worked and talked, and eventually went to sleep.

It took a little more than five hours until Alika inserted the final "key" ceiling block and a low tunnel was built. Alika cut an air vent in the room's ceiling. Then he packed loose snow around the outside seams to make them airtight. The final touch was to spread the caribou mattresses on the sleeping and cooking platform. If it appeared they'd be staying longer than a few days, he'd cut a window space and fill it with clear sea ice to let moonlight in.

Alika and Sulu looked at the house with pride. "Papa might have made it more quickly," Alika said to Sulu.

Sulu nodded. "We did a good job."

Alika said, "Before you were born and the *Reliance* wrecked, we lived in snowhouses that were connected with tunnels."

"Mama told me that," Sulu said.

"There were five neighbors where we lived, and we could visit back and forth without going outside. It was fun."

The two snowhouses, separated by about a hundred feet, were like two large white knobs on the uneven surface of the floe.

At last they sat on the sledge to eat, looking toward shore and the lonely white tundra that slid into the horizon, seeming much closer than it was. Out there on land this time of year were foxes, lemmings, hares, wolves, musk oxen and caribou, falcons, ravens, and snowy owls, but few humans. Most of the bears remained around the ice where the seals lived, sometimes riding floes like this one. How many bears, Alika couldn't guess.

"Do you think Papa and Mama are coming today?" Sulu repeated anxiously, his small face almost hidden in the parka hood.

Alika said, "Let's hope so, Little One." A rescue was doubtful.

"Will the Moon-man help us?" Sulu asked.

"Yes," Alika replied. "He will see us down here and take pity on us and give us especially bright light." Tatkret was always helpful.

Sulu nodded.

If their parents did not show up soon to track the floe, locate it, board it, the boys might be too far down the strait and the darkness day and night would hide them, Alika knew. He couldn't speak of those possibilities. He had to be cheerful, positive, and protective, assuming the ways of the hunter. Alika did think of himself as a grown hunter.

"What is Mama doing now?" Sulu asked. It was a simple question that would probably be asked many times. Alika would have to reply each time.

"Oh, maybe stringing caribou sinew for thread; maybe cooking a rabbit stew; maybe thawing summer berries for us to eat when we come home."

Then the look on Sulu's face told him he was saying wrong things again, reminding his brother of their predicament. Finished eating, he said quickly, "Let's go get a seal."

Alika guessed there were at least a dozen seal breathing-holes within five hundred feet of the house. The problem was finding them beneath the new snow. The air holes were tiny, no more than three inches across. A northwest wind was best for hunting, elders said. But nothing was blowing this morning.

Jamka went about his job without being asked, tail wagging happily. He always seemed to take pleasure in finding an active hole, or one he thought was active, so Alika and his papa could take up watching it.

Sulu by his side, Alika stayed by Jamka's selected hole for more than an hour and then ran out of patience. "Let's see how large the floe is," he said.

He carried the loaded rifle in case a bear showed up. His papa had told him long ago, "Always make sure you kill it with your first shot. A wounded bear, especially a mother with cubs, is the worst enemy a hunter can have. They are deadly."

The boys and dog went north on the floe. Alika wanted to take another look at the berg that had rammed them. It was a giant ship of glacier ice, most of it beneath the water.

Above the water, nearing the top, were large swords of ice pointing skyward. Papa had said there were bad spirits in there, invisible ice people living in the bergs. The berg seemed almost human, a crystal monster without eyes or a mouth. It was already frozen to the floe.

Looking at it, Alika felt sudden rage.

He'd seen bergs out in the strait, glistening in the

sun or menacing under gray clouds. He'd always been frightened by them.

"I'd like to chop it up," he said to Sulu. But that didn't make sense. "Let's go."

To the south as far as Alika could see, the floe ice around them was of varying thickness, with thinly snow-covered mounds, the high hummocks, and the flat parts sometimes five feet above the level of the water. Here and there were deep cracks. Gale winds had blown some of the snow away, leaving shining bare ice. They'd slip and slide on it. The surface of the floe was one of the worst Alika had ever seen.

In what limited, ashen light remained, Alika, Sulu, and Jamka began walking south along the western edge of the floe. Alika thought it would be wiser to take that route rather than getting lost during this first exploration. Soon, scant daylight would fade almost entirely, and exploring would be too dangerous except during full moon. The first few feeble signs of returning light might not happen until late December. Even then the blackness would sometimes be so thick, they wouldn't be able to see each other fifty feet apart.

Alika carried the Maynard percussion carbine at the ready. When his papa had traded a bearskin for this breech-loading rifle, he also got several hundred cartridges, and they had been used sparingly. Alika put three more bullets in his parka.

Sulu had watched his brother handling the rifle and asked, "Do you think we'll meet a bear?" He was uneasy.

"I hope not," Alika answered. "But I'm sure they're here." Sooner or later they were bound to encounter one.

Jamka between them, Alika and Sulu began walking. They had gone about two miles when they heard the bellowing of walrus in the distance. The huge tusked animals, some much heavier than the biggest bears, often herded together in great numbers. They were the only natural enemies of *nanuk*, but the bears seldom challenged the walrus bulls, which had sharp three-foot twin tusks and armorlike skin on their necks and shoulders. Walrus were even better swimmers than bears and could dive to three hundred feet to locate clams and other shellfish on the bottom. Sometimes they attacked kayaking hunters. The only animal that could best a walrus in the water was a killer whale. The killers, merciless, also went after hunters on rare occasions. When the sun was bright, the whales would burst through the ice, attacking the shadows of the horrified hunters in their kayaks above.

Alika said, "Hear that bellowing? I think we're going to see a bear, Little One."

"That's why the walrus are making the noises?"

"I think so."

When they got closer, Alika could see that a huge bear was getting ready to attack the herd, causing all the commotion. He'd seen an attack once before and steered Sulu and Jamka, growling and tense, behind a hummock to watch. Falcons were flying overhead, adding to the grim scene that Alika knew would turn bloody within a few minutes.

Hundreds of walrus were clustered together at the water's edge, with their babies. The bellows shattered the silence. The tusks of the bulls looked like white knives against their rubbery blue-black hides, some of which were blotched with reds and pinks and browns.

"I don't like this," Sulu said. His hand clasped Alika's arm.

"I don't, either, Sulu," said Alika, heart beating fast.

The bear selected his prey, a baby, with care and snatched it up as it shrieked pitifully. The bear dove into the water, away from the raging bulls, and swam with the baby wriggling in his jaws for several hundred yards. Then he climbed back out on the ice, mauling the baby and tossing it playfully before finally killing it with a single bite.

The terror in Sulu's face told Alika he should quickly take his brother away from this savagery. On the other hand, perhaps it was good for the Little One. He'd seen *nanuk,* never afraid of man or animal, as pure predator this afternoon and would remember these moments if he ever had the bad luck to meet a bear face-to-black-nose.

Sulu said, "I never want to see that again." His eyes mirrored his words.

"I hope you don't," Alika said. But if his brother changed and grew up to be a hunter, it was likely the scene would be repeated.

They walked back along the floe edge to the two *iglus,* and Alika tried another seal hole for a little while until full darkness descended. There was still enough emergency food in the small *iglu* to last them a few days. With luck, by then Alika would have harpooned a seal and skinned it. Then they'd have enough blubber and meat to last a few weeks, enough oil to burn for cooking, light, and heat.

That night Alika again thought about the berg that had rammed them. Perhaps it was Kokotah, an evil spirit of the ice cap and enemy of the Inuit, who had guided it.

Big bergs have a bluish tint. Smaller ones that split off are called growlers and are low in the water, indigo in color, awash like a whale's back. Bergs are sometimes locked in pack ice.

5

Mock moons—three bright smaller moonlike spots on lunar halos, seen only in the Arctic during winter—were out in the clear sky, the moon itself staying just a few degrees above the summit of the far western mountains. The mock moons surrounded the moon, which circled the horizon for days this time of year.

Inside the large community hall, a drum was being struck. The shaman Inu would soon speak. Most of the caribou hunters had returned earlier in the day.

Kussu and Maja had visited Inu twice, asking him to help find their sons. "You are now our only hope," Maja had pleaded, her face drawn and weary.

The villagers always came out when Inu spoke his words of wisdom. Inuit believed that the powerful spirits, *tuungait,* could be influenced only by a shaman. The shamans worked with the supernatural and had their own secret language. Inu spent most of his time searching for stolen souls and fighting bad spirits, the people were told.

What made Inu most special was that he could communicate with his polar bear spirit, his *tornaq.* He had gone to the moon and back with his *tornaq,* and had even talked with the long-dead Inuit hunters who lived in the skies.

Inu wore a caribou-skin headband, and a caribou pouch hung from his long neck. No one knew what secrets were hidden in the pouch. Around his waist was a belt of wolf teeth. If bad spirits were attacking the village, he might wear a hideous mask made of whalebone. The people of Nunatak were afraid of Inu's powers, but he did seem able to cure certain illnesses, and he could communicate with the animals and birds, especially bears and ravens. His raven, Punna, was always at his side. It was said that they talked back and forth when alone.

There were good spirits and bad spirits living with the Inuit. The very worst were the *tupilait.* They were evil liars and could cause illness and pain. If a good shaman like Inu caught them, he would end up covered with blood, and only the urine of a musk ox could wash it away.

The flickering blue flame of the large oil lamp lit Inu's long, narrow face, smooth despite his years. He had a white goatee, and it was said his eyes were capable of seeing through stone.

Kussu and Maja sat with the others on the musk ox carpeting, waiting for Inu to speak. Maja chewed on sealskin, which she had planned to use to make summer trousers for Alika and Sulu. Feeble Miak had stopped by in the late afternoon to explain again how he'd survived on his floe many years before. He'd told and retold that story constantly in the village. It was the only memory he had that was substantial. Everyone in the village remained concerned about Alika, Sulu, and Jamka. Like Miak, they'd come by Kussu's dwelling to offer their concerns and thoughts. They all knew the dangers of a drifting floe.

The drumbeater had finished, and Inu, looking directly at Kussu and Maja, said, "They are alive, along with Jamka. They have built an *iglu* and are safe. I can see them..." The silence of the people was as full as that of the mock moons.

Miak, his chin whiskers white and his lips quivering from old age, shouted from the packed audience of eighty-one men, women, and children, "I told you so!"

"Hush, Miak," Kussu said.

Inu spoke again. "The dangers they face are *nanuk* and hunger. I do not know how many bears are on the floe with them, but Jamka is there to warn them. As you know, the farther they drift south, the scarcer seals will become. Alika must try to kill foxes and birds, the dovekies and ptarmigan, with arrows. They should not starve, no matter how long they have to sail."

Miak insisted on interrupting. "I was down to eating pieces of my clothing before rescue!" he called out. Hunters in the Arctic, unable to find any game, were occasionally forced to eat pieces of the skins that covered their bodies. They ate sealskin ropes. It was a last resort.

Miak continued, "Pieces of the floe kept coming off as I went south, until I was sitting on ice no bigger than three musk oxen..."

Inu, eyes as sharp as lance points, said, "Be quiet, Miak. Nuliajuk will take care of them. I promise she will."

Nuliajuk was the goddess of the sea. She was half woman and half fish, and she could communicate with bears, seals, walrus, and all the fish.

When they heard Inu talk of Nuliajuk, Kussu and Maja smiled widely. If the queen of the sea was watching over Alika and Sulu, they would survive.

The beat of the drum was measured and slow as Inu went into his prayer stance. In the most common séance, the shaman summoned his spirits and questioned them. It was said that when he was alone, he could go underground or take flight to the moon. Punna always went with him. He could also go to other lands in the sky. The people of Nunatak believed all this was possible.

When he came out of his prayer stance, Inu said to Kussu, "You must make one last effort to find them. You must take the *umiak* and paddle south with your neighbors and search for them before another gale reaches us."

There was immediate response from the men, even though most had just returned that day from the caribou hunt, and the big skin-boat was launched with twelve paddlers. Shooting stars crossed the sky above, sometimes forming a silver thread from the point where one first appeared until it faded out. Kussu thought they might have luck in finding the boys. He was certain Inu had summoned the shooting stars.

In the Greenland Strait above the Arctic Circle is slush ice, rind ice, cake ice. There is land-fast floe-edge ice, sometimes an ice foot along the edge of the shores, and glacier ice tongues; fields of pack ice a hundred miles square. There is broken sea ice, sometimes submerged, honeycombed and rotten.

6

"I'm so scared," Sulu said.

"About that bear?" Alika asked.

"Yes."

Supper over, the flame in the *qulliq* extinguished, they were on the sleeping platform with Jamka. A thin shaft of moonlight was shining down from the new ice window.

"I am, too," Alika admitted. They'd talked about the baby walrus and the bloody violence of the bear as they walked back to the snowhouse. It was not a memory that would soon go away.

"How many *nanuk* are out here?" Sulu asked.

"I don't know, but I want them to stay away," Alika replied.

Sulu, rubbing Jamka's back, said, "We're lucky to

have him. He'll always warn us if *nanuk* comes, won't he?

"Yes, always."

"I think we should give Jamka more meat so he's always strong and can fight *nanuk*."

"That's a good idea, Sulu," Alika said with a smile.

The polar bear was as much a part of Inuit life as the seal. In the very darkest part of the winter, Papa sometimes talked about *nanuk* while he carved a knife of walrus tusk or a spoon from musk ox horn. Mama would sit and listen while chewing on sealskin.

From Papa and the other hunters, Alika had learned a lot about *nanuk,* the royalty of the Arctic. The bears lived much of the year on the sea ice and gave birth to their cubs in snowdrift dens on land. As well as respecting the bears, all Inuit were afraid of them.

Over the years, Alika had seen a few lumbering along the floe edges in the distance. He had run, fearing they'd scent him. Outside his family's dwelling, buried in snow much of the year, were five honored skulls of bears his papa had killed. The skulls warned other roaming bears not to intrude. So the boys had grown up with reminders of *nanuk*.

Alika knew that with its thick fur, huge paws,

small ears, and stubby tail, a bear could weigh up to fifteen hundred *kabloona* pounds. They were once brown in color, legend said, but became white to blend in with the snow and ice. They dated back millions of winters, Alika had heard.

Alika and Sulu liked the old stories about *nanuk* best, particularly the ones passed down from the *illupiruq,* the great-grandparents. The boys asked the same things over and over. Papa answered each time as if the questions were new. Mama often nodded.

When the hunters of Nunatak gathered together in the long darkness, Alika and Sulu listened with the other villagers. The stories were often about *nanuk* and the old times when the people speared the great white nomad, the times before guns. They always spoke of *nanuk* with reverence. When they killed *nanuk,* they asked for forgiveness. When they escaped his wrath and were not eaten alive, they thanked him.

Old Sipsu said, "A hungry bear kept me inside my hunting *iglu* for five days until I used my knife to dig out the back of it. The bear chased me and took off part of my leg and was ready to chew the rest of me until I stabbed his nose. My mama made a clean cut of my stump and my papa made a crutch to replace the part that *nanuk* had eaten."

Old Arutaq laughed when he talked about out-running bears, but everyone knew he had been paralyzed the one time *nanuk* had surprised him at a seal hole. He'd jammed his spear into the bear's black nose and taken off across the floe. Sulu had laughed long about that, imagining what bowlegged Arutaq had looked like running away.

Then Appa told of being out in his kayak, trying to spear a beluga whale, when *nanuk* swam up from behind, more interested in him than the whale.

There were many stories like these passed down by the brave men who hunted *nanuk* with spears and dogs on open ice.

As Alika and Sulu lay together on their sleeping platform in the dark, Sulu said, "Tell me all the old stories again."

Alika said, "Well, animals ruled the lands everywhere, thousands and thousands of winters ago, well before the first two-legged hunter was born. Caribou and musk oxen were ten feet tall back then. Other animals were even larger than icebergs, with tails twenty feet long."

"Where are they now?" Sulu asked.

"They've been dead a long, long, long time."

"How long?" Sulu asked.

"I don't know," Alika answered. "But as time went by, *nanuk* became smaller, as did the caribou and the musk oxen, the size we have today."

Sulu said, "Why don't the caribou and musk oxen have souls like bears?"

"I think they do," said Alika. "Maybe Inu knows for sure. But I do know about the souls of bears. Papa always made certain that the souls of the ones he killed were satisfied and went to *nanuk* heaven. He smeared caribou fat on their mouths and hung his lance over their heads for five days. He would not kill another bear for many months, and that satisfied their souls."

Both Alika and Sulu knew about Papa's fight with one bear before they were born. He had been gone three days and came home with the *nanuk* carcass on his sledge and with frightful wounds on his back. They'd seen his scars. He'd shared the bear meat with the whole village.

Sulu said, "Is it true what Inu has said, that bears can hear us talk?"

"I think so," Alika answered. Inu would not say what wasn't true.

"After they are dead, can they hear us talk?"

"Their souls can. They never really die," Alika said.

Sulu said, "When Papa killed his last bear, he put its skull over in a corner and Mama decorated it with beads. Why?"

"To make its spirit happy. Inu said to always do that."

Sulu asked, "How does Inu know so much about the spirits of the bears?"

"Because Inu has been to bear country on the other side of the moon. Like I said, the soul of the bear, the *tornaq,* does not die with the body," Alika said.

Sulu asked, "Do you think *nanuk* is part human?"

"It is said that when the bears are in their own houses, they are naked like us, but they put their hides back on when they go outside."

Sulu asked, "Is it true that long ago *nanuk* took turns being human and even married humans?"

Alika nodded. "They are much like us. As you know, they can stand on their hind legs, sit down or lean against a hummock. You know the skinned carcass of the bear resembles our bodies. Think about that, Sulu."

Sulu asked, "Is there any time of the year when *nanuk* is more dangerous?"

Alika replied, "It all depends on the food supply. One time before you were born, the seals just disappeared. No one knows why they swam away, but the bears were starving and so were we. Then some of the bears came to our village, and Papa stood guard and shot them. It was their survival or ours."

Sulu asked, "What makes the bear so dangerous?"

"Papa said that the thin bear is always more dangerous than the fat bear. It is only hunger that causes them to attack humans. I think they are the most dangerous in late summer, when the water is still open and they haven't had many meals. Remember Jimi?"

"Yes."

A bear had come into the village and carried Jimi away. He was ten years old, the same age as Sulu. His remains were found two miles from the dwellings, causing much sorrow as well as fright.

"I hope that doesn't happen to us," Sulu said. "A bear eating me!"

"Papa always told us to stay away from *nanuk* until we are very experienced hunters. And we must never mistake its speed. It looks slow when it walks along, but an eyeblink will show you just how fast it can run. Suddenly, those jaws that can take an arm off have you by the shoulder. But remember this, Sulu: The bear will let off a slight puff of air before it attacks. If you hear it, shoot. This has happened to Papa a few times. The bear surprised him, and he heard the soft puffs. One time the bear was only five arm-lengths away. Hungry bears will stalk you and come up behind you."

Sulu said, "I will run."

Alika said, "You'd better run very fast."

Sulu yawned.

"Go to sleep now, Sulu."

"I will. Thank you for talking." Then he added, "Someday I'll carve a bear of ivory and give it to you." Papa had three walrus tusks waiting for that day. Teacher Etukak would not permit ivory for a while. Sulu could use only soapstone or wood.

Alika said, "I know it will be beautiful. Now go to sleep."

Newborn bergs can be five hundred feet high and reach twice as deep underwater. A berg fifty to a hundred feet high may have swordlike spikes on its face because of the way it has melted.

7

In the middle of the strait, more than fifty miles below Nunatak, Alika, Sulu, and Jamka stood in front of their new home as they floated slowly along. They were looking up at the mock moons. They had seen these friendly moons many times before, but they still watched them because they'd been told the spirits had planted them up there especially for Inuit eyes.

There were times when the circling moon was visible, but the surrounding small ones were missing. Alika and Sulu wondered where they had gone and why. Inu had once said the small missing moons were asleep below the horizon and would return to be with the moon after they rested.

Soon, Alika and Sulu crawled down the low entrance tunnel, barely two feet high, followed by

Jamka. Then Alika placed a block of hard snow in the tunnel to ward off any wind that might come up. Jamka would again nestle between them in the dank chill. The bedding was already on the sleeping platform. Jamka would get the usual prod in the ribs if he snored, which he often did.

Sulu lay silent for a while, then said, "Papa did not rescue us today. Where was he?"

"I'm sure he tried if he thought we were still near home."

Silence again from Sulu, then, "Will we die out here?"

"Not unless I make mistakes."

"What kind of mistakes?"

"Fall off the ice and into the water. Get us mixed up with a bear." It would be easy enough to slip-slide down a hummock and fall in.

"How long will we have to stay out here?" Sulu asked.

Good question! Alika had a choice of two answers: He didn't know how long, or he could suggest they might drift over to Greenland. He chose the latter. Give Sulu some hope.

"I'd like that," Sulu said.

"So would I," said Alika.

Sulu was thoughtful again for a few minutes, then asked, "Why did we leave Grandmother Maani to die?"

Alika was surprised. Where had this question come from?

The family had been hunting toward the mountains last spring. There was snow nearby. Grandmother Maani was very old, and she told them it was her time to go. Then she sat in the middle of a small *iglu* as the family built it around her, without an entry tunnel. She closed her eyes as the last block was placed, and the family said words to her spirit and then they went on their way. It was Inuit tradition for the elderly to die alone, with no one nearby to interfere with their spirits. The family returned in five full moons to bury her body in rocks. Burial was never in the frozen earth.

Alika said, "That was how she wanted it—one less mouth to feed."

Sulu was silent again, then asked about Nanuki, once more thinking of death.

Nanuki had died of something wrong with his stomach four winters ago. He was wrapped in skins and dragged up a hillside on his sledge. He was then placed in a sitting position in a big rock hole, with his face to the west and all of his personal possessions laid out around him. Sulu had seen the procession, Alika remembered. During the ceremony, the women expressed their sorrow by inserting a small bunch of dried grass into their left nostrils, and the men inserted grass into their right nostrils.

"That's enough thinking about death, Little One."

Jamka had begun to snore again, and Alika poked him.

Sulu asked, "What shall we name our ship of ice?"

"I have no idea," Alika answered. What would his brother think of next? "You decide." Sulu was full of surprises.

"What about *Polar Star*?"

"*Polar Star*. That's a good name," said Alika. The spirits would approve.

There was silence for another few minutes. Then Sulu said, "I need to keep talking."

"About what now?"

"Anything. I can't stand this terrible silence." No wind was blowing.

Alika sighed. He shook his head in frustration and tried to think of something else to talk about. Sulu had been on caribou hunts with their parents and other villagers.

Alika blew out an exasperated breath. "Caribou live on our tundra all year. They have round hooves so they can walk more easily on the snow. Some of our caribou go south, swimming rivers after the thaw. Others go up to the tree line to winter. They dig through the snow for plants to feed on."

"Tell me about wolves," Sulu insisted.

Alika said tiredly, "Wolves move with the caribou herds. The caribou know the wolves are there and can do nothing about it. A wolf picks out a single caribou, and the caribou cannot escape. The wolf rushes, leaping at the caribou's neck and tearing it open. The wolf feasts on the raw meat while the caribou herd moves on. Then the ravens feast."

Sulu said, "I've seen it."

"Then you didn't need me to tell about it."

Sulu said, "I know."

The night would never be solid black. Even in the middle of winter, there was always faint light below the southern horizon. And each month there was always the reflection of the snow, the northern lights, and the familiar moon shining down to comfort the Inuit.

8

For almost an hour, in the scant midday twilight, Jamka had been sniffing for seal holes at the ice edge. Alika and Sulu followed him thirty or forty feet away. Alika knew the rhythms of the winter seal, which began at the end of summer when the ice was new. As the temperature dropped and the ice thickened, the seal repeated its underwater mining to keep the vertical breathing tunnels open. Finally, the dog found a hole he thought was active. He dug down in a flurry of white until he exposed the small opening.

All Inuit children grew up knowing that without seals, their people could not live in the Arctic. Hunters only killed them for skins and food so they could walk in warmth with a full belly. As it said in an old Inuit poem:

Nuliajuk, great goddess of mankind,
Send us the seals
So that we may have food,
And fat,
And clothing.

Beasts of the sea,
Come offer yourself
In the cold, clear light
Of the morning.

One thing that Alika did not have to worry about was his harpoon. It was believed that seals and other animals resented being killed by shoddy harpoons or spears or knives, and if they were, they told their souls. The souls then warned other animals. But Papa's weapons were works of art that would never cause a seal to resent its death. And Alika always wore a small seal, carved out of wood by Sulu, for a good-luck charm.

He sat on his square of bear hide, wriggling his toes to keep them warm. "I hope the clouds will move east so I can hunt tonight by the moonlight."

Sulu sat on another square nearby. He said, "I dreamt about birds last night."

There was nothing unusual about that, Alika thought.

"First, a raven, over the horizon, caught the smell of that baby walrus the bear killed and went after the remains the bear left, pecking the white fox again and again until it gave up."

Alika laughed. "That's one tough bird." Only the snowy owl was as tough.

"The next dream I had, you were with me. There was a horned lark being chased by a falcon..."

Suddenly the indicator rod jigged, and Jamka stiffened and bent forward. A seal's bullet-shaped head appeared, and Alika drove the harpoon lance into it just below the right eye, grabbing the attached rope with his left hand. The animal struggled in a death dance but could not get away.

Alika yelled in triumph and Jamka howled loudly. Sulu shouted, "You did it, brother!"

Alika sat down in the snow by the fresh kill, exhausted more from the long watch than from the short struggle. He knew he was lucky. Once, when the family was almost starving, Papa had stayed by a hole for nearly forty-eight hours before making a kill.

If this could happen every week, they'd survive. Alika felt good. He said to Sulu, "I'll butcher it now and scrape the skin tomorrow or the next day." He'd watched his mama many times with the *ulu,* the very sharp woman's knife. Other knives were used to prepare the skin for drying.

Jamka, eyes fastened on the seal carcass, sat a few feet away. He would follow every move until he got some meat.

Wanting Sulu to be involved in everything, to keep his mind occupied, Alika said, "Get the knife for me."

Meanwhile, he rolled the seal onto its back. It was fat and healthy, fully grown. "And get me the freshwater bag." The walrus-intestine bag was wrapped in one of the musk ox hides so it wouldn't freeze. In a gesture to the spirit of the dead seal, Alika poured a little water into its mouth, blessing the animal for the gift of its body.

A few minutes later, holding a front flipper, he cut around at the bottom of it, through a layer of fat down to the meat. Then he did the same thing to the other flipper, the tail flipper, and the head. From the head, he slit the belly to the tail, through the layer of greasy blubber to the stomach, and continued to separate the blubber from the meat, lifting the skin. Finally, he made cuts through to the ribs and spine, preserving the all-important skin. It took him longer than it would have taken Mama, but the results were the same.

Jamka was almost drooling, waiting for his share. Of course he'd be rewarded for finding the proper *aglus.*

"It won't be long," Sulu said happily.

The beat of wings approaching low overhead in the final moments of the noon twilight made them look up as a pair of ravens crossed the sky. Some said the black birds were good luck; others said they were omens of evil.

Sulu shouted, "We'll be rescued!" He was one who believed ravens were good luck.

"Or the wind will blow us ashore," said Alika with joy as the wing beats faded.

The boys took some of the meat into the snow-house and stored the rest, along with the skin and bones, in the smaller *iglu.* Then Alika used the bow drill, with a few fingers of dried moss, to start the cooking fire. Jamka preferred his meat raw.

They would boil the meat, along with the heart, stomach, flippers, and head. The intestines would be cleaned of digested food, squeezed out, and washed in freshwater. The liver could be eaten raw or cooked. The blubber would melt into oil. They soon ate.

It had been a successful day, and now it was time to sleep. The odor of the cooked meat lingered in the snowhouse, reminding both Alika and Sulu of their own home and how good life was there with Mama cooking and Papa telling stories, singing the old songs, sometimes beating on the drum.

Jamka was again in the middle on the sleeping platform, a slice of moonlight shining down on them through the window. After a silence, Sulu asked, "What will happen to me if something happens to you?"

Alika said, "Nothing is going to happen to either of us. If the wind blows hard enough, it will push us over to Greenland. We'll go ashore, someone will give us a kayak, and I'll paddle us home."

"Home is a long way," said Sulu.

It seemed to Alika that Sulu thought only of home. "I know, but I can do it."

The northwest wind, the woman's wind, sometimes blew hard in late October and November. Blizzards were sometimes pushed by the woman's wind, but it could also push the floe eastward.

Outside, the night remained clear and calm. The ghostly northern lights, the aurora borealis, flickered here and there in colored patterns, sending a mysterious message to all who lived in the Arctic. Inu had said the lights were controlled by the spirits.

Reds, greens, and purples collapsed in veiled swirls and vanished. Then streamers of pale green turned to ivory. Soon there were folds of violets and blues that quivered and danced. Inu had said the lights were the spirits of people who had died from loss of blood—wounds, childbirth, murder. Inu called them *aqsarniit*. Deeply fearing the aurora, the Inuit went into their huts when the lights were in the sky.

Alika and Sulu had seen the beginning of the heavenly show before entering their home to sleep. Had they been outside, they would have sworn they again heard whistling and crackling noises in the distance and would have been frightened by them as usual. But an hour had passed and Sulu was asleep. Jamka was dreaming, probably chasing a caribou across the tundra, his legs twitching. Only Alika was awake, looking at the colors through the ice-pane window of the snowhouse.

There were many glaciers on the north coast of
Ellesmere Island in the direction of the North Pole,
and the largest ice shelves of the continent were up there.
The shelves were ancient deposits of freshwater,
sometimes fifty or more feet deep.

9

In the morning, Alika awakened first. He soon crawled outside, Jamka at his heels. In the moonlight, he saw that the short tunnel to the storage *iglu* had been smashed and knew immediately that a bear had visited while they'd slept.

"Where is it?" he asked Jamka. He'd made a mistake, he knew, storing the seal remains out there.

The dog was already sniffing the subzero air. The bear would have had its fill, and the always-following white fox was likely dining on whatever was left. It was the scent of the white fox, not far away, that Jamka followed. There was no bloody trail on the snow because the seal remains were frozen, but Alika did see some drag marks from both the bear's paws and the seal's body. He lifted the rifle out of the snow just in case *nanuk* was still close by.

Jamka moved swiftly, Alika squinting after him. Then Jamka howled, signaling that the fox was gone and that he was guarding the seal remains. The bear must not have been too hungry or it would have devoured every ounce of the seal, Alika thought. There would have been a different tone to Jamka's howl if the bear were near.

Alika went into the storage *iglu* for seal rope to drag home whatever meat, bone, and skin was left. Then, gripping the rifle, he joined Jamka, hitched up the *nattiq* remains, and trudged back to the snowhouse. Alika would have to admit to Sulu that they were in deep trouble. Unless he soon killed another seal, they would be out of food as well as blubber for heat and cooking and light.

Returning inside the *iglu,* Alika saw that his brother was awake, and he told him that a bear had robbed them of the seal carcass. "There is enough left for three days if we eat only once a day."

Sulu couldn't believe what had happened. "You mean that bear stole our food?"

"He has only one job. That's to feed himself," Alika answered. "Get dressed. We're going hunting."

Sulu asked, "Why didn't you bring the meat in here last night?" He was frowning.

"I didn't think about it. From now on I will."

"Why didn't Jamka smell the bear?"

Alika replied, "He's not perfect, either."

Sulu got dressed, and they went together toward the east side of the floe.

Alika had not noticed the sharpness of the stars the night before and had no idea that a blizzard was moving rapidly westward. They were roughly five miles away from the snowhouse when the wind began to howl and the first thick pellets of snow filled the air. The wind was blowing probably forty miles an hour.

"We have to go back!" Alika shouted to Sulu. "Stay near me."

He had no compass except Jamka, but he'd been caught out in storms several times with Papa. They'd located boulders to hide behind on the tundra and had used the dog team as a barrier, packing the dogs close together, burying themselves behind them in the snow.

Papa had also taught him how, in certain circumstances, he could navigate by snowdrifts. Blizzard snow, though soft, is thick, and the navigator waits until the storm is over to read the tonguelike drifts and decide in which direction the wind had blown. But often, evil Oqaloraq, the snowdrift spirit, attempts to harm the hunters by confusing them while they struggle home.

There were no boulders on the floe, but Alika remembered several ice hummocks they'd passed midmorning, one of which ran east and west and looked to be about twenty feet high. If he could find it, they might survive huddling behind it and hoping that the storm would be short-lived.

In the meantime, Alika yelled to Jamka, "Take us home!"

Bent into the wind and snow, heads down, trying to follow Jamka's tail, they slogged and slipped across the ice for almost two hours in what Alika thought was a westerly direction. Alika kept saying encouraging words to an exhausted Sulu but finally gave up and slung his brother across his shoulders. The snow was coming in gusts. To carry Sulu, Alika had no choice but to drop the rifle. He planted the harpoon in the snow to mark the spot.

They had stopped several times to rest, hands and feet almost numb, and Alika was nearing exhaustion himself when he saw the dim shape of the big hummock ahead through the flakes. He remembered it wasn't too far from the snowhouse and yelled to Jamka, "Keep going!"

They made it home, and gathering strength, Alika dragged Sulu into the tunnel, saying, "Brother, the spirits looked down on us." He knew their hands and faces were frostbitten, but they were alive and that's what counted. Painful as frostbite was, they could deal with it by letting the parts thaw naturally. The extreme cold had bitten him before.

He fired up the *qulliq,* undressed Sulu, who was moaning, inserted him into his sleeping bag, and promised himself they'd never leave their side of the floe again. When the weather changed, he'd go back and pick up the rifle.

Jamka had shaken the snow off his fur outside, but his coat was still damp. He was already up beside Sulu, and Alika joined them, fatigue and fear having drained him. Before falling asleep, he made another promise to himself: Always check the weather signs.

He retrieved the Maynard the next morning.

Freezing of the sea ice is an amazing process. It can take place with startling rapidity. One day, a hunter may use his kayak for travel. The next day, he can walk across the same water, then frozen.

10

The blizzard gripped Nunatak, east wind driving the snow.

"I can't sleep despite Inu telling us that they are alive and well. Just the idea that they are trapped out there in this weather frightens me," said Maja from their raised wooden sleeping platform.

"I did what Inu told me to do—you know that. I got all the hunters together in the big boat and we paddled south all night but couldn't find them."

"It was too late," Maja said with despair.

"You must trust in Alika," Kussu said.

"Suppose he has fallen into the water, leaving Sulu to survive alone? Suppose they are out in this storm?"

Kussu said, "I have taught Alika to be very careful on the ice, and he knows bad weather. I took him hunting with me on his third birthday; remember? I can't count the number of times he has been with me ever since."

"If it wasn't for this storm and darkness, we could take the dogs and follow the shore south," Maja said. "That floe could have grounded."

"Many things would be different in our lives if it wasn't for this darkness," Kussu said.

"We should live where there is light," she said angrily. "They may be starving."

Kussu said, "They can hunt on the nights before the full moon and during it and the nights just after it. We've done it. That's what Alika will do. He will use that light to sit by a hole and wait."

Both had indeed done it. On the nights of the moon, without any cloud cover, it almost became like daylight. Snow glistened.

"Suppose he does not get a seal on one of those nights?"

Kussu said, "He will."

It was now mid-November, black outside, forty degrees below zero. Maja said, "I keep thinking about them huddled in darkness without light or heat."

Kussu, seeking the right words, finally answered. "You keep talking about all the bad things that can happen to them. I believe that Alika is learning something new every day. Jamka will find the holes, and Alika will kill the seals. Believe me."

Maja said, "Have you asked Miak at what point south his floe began to break into small pieces? As soon as some light begins to return, we can go there and find our boys."

"I will ask him."

"No matter how far south," Maja said in a demanding voice.

"No matter how far south," Kussu agreed, though he said it without conviction.

From what Kussu knew about the Greenland Strait and the many fjords and inlets and islands to the south, they would have to use their kayaks to cross open waters once the ice melted. But that would be months ahead. They would walk and carry their kayaks when necessary, and they'd kill game along the way for food. They knew the names of several of the villages in the south.

Maja said forcefully, "We will do it, husband."

He answered, "Yes, we will."

They embraced.

Kussu knew that what the boys' mother proposed was impossible. He'd seen a nautical chart of the Arctic coast on the *Reliance*. With its inlets and islands and rivers for a thousand miles south, the only way to rescue his sons was to empty the village of all males and paddle an *umiak* until they reached the boys—if they were alive. It would take weeks, and Kussu knew he could not ask the hunters of Nunatak to be away from their work and families that long.

Maja was not satisfied. She would not sleep soundly or pass a day with peace of mind until her sons were rescued.

For more than two thousand years, dogs
have pulled wooden sleds across the Arctic ice, snow,
and summer tundra, providing work, comfort,
hunting skills, and sniffing abilities.

11

Alika was at a seal hole with Sulu, not far from the snowhouse. Jamka was guarding the hole when there was a sound of ice shattering about a hundred feet away. Pieces flew into the air as the entire body of a narwhal shot up, twisting and turning. Its ten-foot tusk was aimed toward the sky. They watched as the narwhal fell back into the opening.

"What was that?" a shaken Sulu asked.

Alika was shaken, too, but finally said, "I think a killer whale was chasing it."

There were no sounds, but Alika knew there was a wild struggle under the ice between the narwhal and the killer whale, and he could only imagine them going at each other in a fight to the death, their huge bodies swimming up and down, circling.

The ripping jaws of the killer whale would have the advantage, he thought.

Blood soon stained the water around the floe edge, and a while later the killer whale floated to the surface, a piece of the narwhal's tusk rammed into its belly.

Sulu asked, "Could they come through the ice after us?"

"I doubt they'd bother," Alika answered, though he was still shaken by the fight. It would be quite a story to tell in the meeting hall when they returned to Nunatak.

Sulu, seeing one of the killer whale's big eyes already beginning to film over, asked, "What else is out here?"

Alika said, "If we drift far enough south, you may see belugas or bowhead whales. But they aren't any threat, Papa said. The belugas talk a lot. I've heard them. They chirp and click to one another. The bowheads have no interest in us."

Sulu wasn't convinced. "Did we do something bad to the spirits? Maybe even Kokotah?"

"Not at all, Little One. We've just had awful luck. I think good things will now start happening."

They stayed by the *aglus* another hour, then Alika gave up waiting and they walked several hundred yards to another hole that Jamka selected.

After an hour with no results, they returned to the snowhouse, ate, and went to bed.

A while later, Alika was awakened by a heavy thump and rolled off the sleeping platform onto the hard-packed floor. Jamka had also been awakened by the strange sound and had jumped down to the floor with a growl. Alika felt the husky's tense body a few inches away and asked, "What was that?" Sulu didn't awaken.

If it had been a bear about to attack, Jamka would have acted on instinct and already gone outside. Alika stayed on his hands and knees for a few minutes longer, trying to think of what might have happened. No human could have caused the thump. If something had hit the snowhouse from above, the snow blocks would have caved in.

The thump had to have been caused by grounding or impact with another big floe or maybe even by a berg ramming them from behind. There were no other possibilities.

Alika whispered to Jamka, "Let's go." His heart

was pounding. They began to crawl out of the windbreak tunnel, Alika's mouth dry with suspense. He picked up the Maynard.

Outside, the moon was struggling to break through the cloud cover, shining for a few seconds and then disappearing. But in the few shafts of light, Alika saw what had caused the thump: A berg, with sky-reaching shards of ice like grinning teeth, had ridden up alongside the floe, temporarily locking to it. Alika was certain it was the same berg that had rammed them before and broken them from land, a familiar berg that seemed to have a grudge against them.

It had also grounded, probably in shallow water, stopping the drift of their floe. Perhaps they could crawl over it? Maybe it was up against the eastern shore and they could just step off onto land and head for home. Alika had never heard of anyone climbing up the slick surface of a berg, though. If only the in-and-out clouds covering the moon would give him a chance to really see it. But they soon thickened.

Alika stayed outside with Jamka, going closer to the berg, until the wind began to whine. Then they returned to the house for safety.

Alika felt his way inside and climbed back onto the sleeping platform, arranging his body along Jamka's back. He lay there thinking about the berg and this chance, maybe the only chance, to escape.

Perhaps on the other side of the berg, he could carry Sulu on his back and wade ashore. Jamka could swim it, of course. But Alika did not know how far the floe had drifted from Nunatak; whether he could go north and find the village in the blackness. And there were other problems. Many.

He didn't know if he could climb the berg with his sealskin boots, which had little traction and often skidded on the flattest ice. Even if he could reach the top, he'd have to figure out a way to get Sulu and Jamka up there.

As soon as Sulu awakened, Alika said, "A berg hit us while you slept. I think it is the same miserable one that rammed us before. It has grounded. I'm going to try to climb to the top of it and see how close we are to shore. Jamka will stay here and guard you."

"Why can't I go along?" Sulu asked, eyes still heavy with sleep.

"I don't want you to fall and hurt yourself. It will be very slippery going up. If there is not much water on the other side, we might be able to escape."

"When will you do it?"

There was dim light coming through the ice-pane window. The storm had passed, and there was enough moonlight still beaming down to make it possible for Alika to navigate the climb.

"I'll try now."

There was a gaff, a carved whalebone hook, still strapped to the sledge from summer sea-fishing. Alika unwound the rope from the short wooden tool, thinking he could use the pole to pull himself up if needed. Sulu followed his brother and Jamka outside, and on seeing the huge shape plastered with new snow and its shards lit up, ran to Alika and grabbed his legs, saying, "Don't do it; please don't do it..."

"It may be our only chance, Little One. The farther south we drift, the more the strait will open wider and the more the floe will begin to crumble. The winter hunters may not come out this far. I must try. Papa and Mama would want me to try."

"I'm so frightened," said Sulu, his small face tight with alarm. "When you get to the top, you could slide down into the water and I'll never see you again. Never!"

"I promise I'll be careful," Alika replied. "Very careful."

The brothers and the dog advanced on the berg, and the closer Alika walked toward it, the more he felt as if this huge mass of ice were saying to him, "Don't you dare!" The wind had blown the new snow away from some of the crevasses chiseled on its ugly frozen face. It was an ancient berg, Alika knew. Perhaps hundreds of glacier winters old.

Alika stood for a few minutes longer looking at the frowning face and trying to work up the courage to make the climb. He wished he could speak to Inu, ask him to provide a good Inuit spirit to help.

He studied the face, carefully examining the entire front of the berg. The swordlike blades of ice here and there had tips that were knife sharp, probably from the summer melt. If he fell on any of them, he'd likely die.

Both Sulu and Jamka had their eyes focused on him. He couldn't turn back. He said to himself, "I have to be strong." *Nukilik.* He hugged Sulu and said to the dog, "You take care of my brother."

Alika stepped off the floe and onto the berg, holding the whalebone hook in his right hand. As a child during the short Arctic summers, he'd scrambled over big rocks in an area south of the village while playing with other boys, but he had never thought he'd have to climb a berg. He wished the storm wind had blown all the snow off the ice so he could see the best way to go up.

The crevasses might be the answer, and Alika edged toward them, his boots already sliding on the slick surface beneath the snow. The ice in the crevasses, hidden from the sun, would be rock hard.

Reaching the first crevasse, he hooked the gaff and pulled himself up. Anything Papa had made could be trusted. And Alika still had the strength to climb. They'd eaten the last piece of raw seal the night before.

He could hear Sulu shouting from below, "Keep going!" And even Jamka howled. Alika was afraid to turn his head to look at them, so instead he pressed his body against the ice, ready to ascend another five feet.

He worked the gaff out of the berg's grasp and hooked it again, another five feet higher, then rested a moment. He kept thinking that if the berg was close to the shore on the other side, it would act as a bridge, even if they had to wade a little. He didn't know how far south the floe had traveled, but being anywhere onshore would be better than continuing to ride it.

Alika took several deep breaths and once more pulled himself up. Sulu shouted, "Don't fall!" Alika decided to go over to the next crevasse, which was wider and sloped more deeply inward.

Five feet at a time, resting after each pull, it took Alika almost half an hour to reach the fortresslike top of the berg. When he looked down the other side, he tried not to weep, but failed. The shore was at least two hundred feet away, an impossible distance to wade. Even if he succeeded, he'd be soaked, and there'd be no way to dry off.

As he stood on top of the berg, the wind dried his tears. He realized it was a useless mission. Any plan for hauling Sulu and Jamka up the icy wall would not have worked. He didn't have even enough strength left to climb it again himself.

He looked around. To the west was endless tundra, no sign of human life; to the east, across the strait, the white mountains of Greenland were outlined in the moonlight.

He stayed atop the berg for a few minutes, then used the gaff to help himself slide down. Finally feeling the floe with his boots, he heard Sulu ask, "Can we go ashore?"

Alika shook his head. "There's too much water on the other side. We're stuck here, Little One."

"I was afraid of that," Sulu said.

"I've got to kill a seal right away," Alika said. The day before he'd seen that Sulu trembled as he walked, from lack of food.

Moonlight was now their only hope.

The next two days, a light wind blew from the northwest, good for hunting, chasing the clouds. The moon was again shining down, and a most beautiful halo encircled it, as bright as Tatkret himself. Horizontal and vertical rays extended from it to form a perfect cross.

Alika had instructed Sulu to stay in the *iglu* and conserve his energy. Meanwhile, Alika spent hours at two different seal holes that Jamka had chosen. At last, on the third night—when Alika had to crawl, because of weakness, to the hole selected by Jamka—a seal rose to the surface for a quick breath, and Alika used the last of his strength to drive the harpoon into its thin skull. Then he found new energy to widen the hole and pull the animal out onto the snow, where it died.

Alika and Jamka teamed to drag the carcass to the snowhouse, Alika shouting, "Sulu, come out here and look at what we have!"

Sulu soon appeared, grinning widely. "I knew you'd do it, big brother."

This time Alika had no freshwater with which to anoint the lips of the seal, and he prayed to the animal's fleeing spirit to allow him this error. He promised he'd never do it again.

Inside the *iglu,* away from any bear's snooping nostrils, he began to use the woman's knife to butcher the seal, saving every drop of warm blood that he could for Sulu, Jamka, and himself. They needed it badly and drank it greedily. In the faint shaft of the moon's light through the ice pane, provided at a lucky angle, Alika skillfully cut the seal, first saving every ounce of the blubber so that he could light the *qulliq.* Later he would boil the meat as needed. But now they ate it raw, slicing the delicious liver into three pieces.

After filling their stomachs, which soon ached from being so stuffed, they went to sleep, Alika and

Sulu thanked the seal and the moon for saving them. There was enough food to last four weeks if they ate very little of it at a time.

In the morning, Alika chopped some ice out of the berg, melted it, and filled the pair of walrus intestines with the freshwater. It could still be obtained on the surface of the floe, but the frozen snow-coated pools of it were difficult to locate.

A week later, a strong gale from the northwest ripped the grounded berg loose from the bottom, and Alika heard the ice cracking and felt the floe move, too. With the wind driving it, the berg would sail on south at a much faster rate than the floe.

It was now late December. They'd managed to survive since mid-October. Alika knew that the sun would faintly return late the next month. Until then the almost constant night would remain.

But this day there was about an hour of twilight at noon. Alika, Sulu, and Jamka stood outside to celebrate. The winter darkness was always bad at home, but there on the drifting ice, it seemed much worse. Any thin sign of light was celebrated.

Then they returned inside and climbed up onto the sleeping platform, and Sulu said, "Tell me about the places where there is day and night during the winter. I want to go there."

"So do I," Alika replied. "But maybe Jamka wouldn't want to come with us."

Sulu laughed and said, "How do we get there?"

"It is too far for our kayaks."

"Tell me about those places anyway," Sulu demanded.

"The year you were born, Papa took me to where the ship was waiting to go to the North Pole," Alika said. "One of us from the village of Iqaluit, far to the south, had been to the places where there was night and day during the winter. He took care of the ship's sledge dogs. He told Papa about warm waters and trees that were called palms. People swam in the warm waters and soaked up the sun on sandy beaches."

Sulu said, "Brother Alika, take me there someday."

"I'll take you there, I promise," Alika answered.

From time to time over the weeks that passed, Alika had thought how lucky he was to have Sulu with him. Now and then, Sulu had pestered him, but Alika couldn't imagine being stranded on the floe without someone to talk to, someone he knew and loved. He loved Jamka, too, and realized that without the husky they already would have died, but having someone to talk to who could talk back was critical.

From time to time on sleepless nights, Alika had thought about old Miak surviving on the drifting ice with no human or dog around. Miak should have gone crazy, should not have survived. But he had killed a bear, Alika remembered, with his harpoon, and the *nanuk* meat had kept him alive for four months. Alika had a dream about old Miak one night, saw him moving around his *iglu*, talking to himself.

Only in the Arctic could humans be trapped on a great mass of ice, drifting on a sea that had no mercy. Yet Miak had been rescued by hunters. Maybe he and Sulu and Jamka would have the same luck.

The Arctic Ocean is perpetually covered
with ice, and a persistent circular current feature,
the Beaufort Gyre, sweeps the sea ice southwestward
along the northwestern coast of Canada.

12

Thick snow, driven by a high wind, attacked the floe for two days. Lighted by the *qulliq,* Alika busied himself scraping meat off the sealskin. Sulu helped. Alika dressed out the flippers of the new seal, saving every morsel. Then he used the *Reliance* ax to cut several lengths of wood off the sledge so Sulu could carve to pass the time.

The storm stopped the second night, while they were asleep. In the morning, with the temperature probably thirty below, Alika saw two sets of bear tracks near the snowhouse and also sighted the everpresent white fox tracks.

"We had visitors last night," he said to Sulu. "Look!"

Sulu said to Jamka, "Why didn't you wake us up?"

"The wind. He didn't smell them."

Sulu said, "You'll have to do better, Jamka."

The bears were likely on the prowl after burrowing down during the storm. Jamka sniffed the tracks but didn't seem disturbed by them. Apparently, the *nanuks* weren't nearby. "Better we stay inside for a while anyway," Alika said.

Then he double-checked the carbine to make certain it was ready for use. There were ice crystals on the barrel, but it cocked easily. Alika well knew that against a charging bear, he'd likely have only one shot. He'd have to depend on Jamka to slow the charge and not get in the way.

To pass time, he resharpened every knife and then began kneading the sealskins, though they'd need sunshine for stretching and softening. What else was there to do? Finally, Alika said, "Let's hunt. I need to get out of here." But Jamka's holes weren't active, and they returned to the *iglu* for another harrowing night.

The wind moaned and, combined with the creaking of the floe—now and then a muffled collision, perhaps a bergy bit crashing against their floe—and the eerie darkness inside the snowhouse, made each hour agonizing. Alika wondered how long they could take it. How many days and nights could they last, not even counting the dangers of the weather and *nanuk*?

Sulu asked, "Will there be another summer for us?"

"Of course," Alika said. But he had no proof. Maybe not even another night?

Sulu said, "I can't wait."

"Just keep thinking about it, brother," Alika said. "Close your eyes and think about all the sunshine. You'll get warm just thinking about it."

All Inuit lived for the spring and summer, delighted in each day and night, especially those who lived north of the Arctic Circle. The sun would stay above the horizon from mid-May until late July, and even though the temperature could dip to thirty below in the spring for a day or two, or snow could fall, those seasons were like heaven to Alika and Sulu and their people.

As the snow disappeared, the tundra would be covered with willow catkins and poppies and buttercups and mountain avens and purple saxifrage and Lapland rosebay and heather. Orange lichen covered the rocks; yellow-green moss filled the

valleys. Huge Arctic bumblebees came out of no-
where to suck nectars. Summer was goodness and
happiness to Alika and Sulu.

In the late winter and spring, occasionally there
were sun dogs, twenty-two degrees on either side of
the sun, caused by airborne ice crystals, sometimes
accompanied by luminous arcs and bands. The Arctic sky, Qilak, was a place of wonder to every Inuit.

Summer was the time of year when the moon
slept. If it could be seen at all, it was the color of pale
white cheese. No stars could be seen. Sun flooded the
northland, and the Inuit collected eggs and hunted
and fished around the clock. Who wanted to waste
the good light and relative warmth bedded down?

Sulu said, "Will I see the birds again?"

Alika said, "Of course."

Sulu's papa and mama had no idea why he had
fallen in love with birds. Neither did Alika.

The only birds that Sulu could see during the
winter were the ravens, the dovekies, the gyrfalcons,
the ptarmigan, and the snowy owls. So Sulu wor-
shiped the flocks of birds that came in the spring and
summer. He couldn't wait each year until the mi-
grating waterbirds were seen, the snow geese and the
ducks, the common eiders and gaudy king eiders,

the red-throated loons, the black guillemots and the piratical, nest-robbing jaegers. Almost thirty different kinds of birds visited during the spring and summer, millions of them. Sulu could identify most. He knew the perching birds as well as the seabirds that skimmed low over the melting ice.

When a peregrine dived on a horned lark, he would shout, "Look out, lark!" When the jaeger plundered the nest of a phalarope, he'd yell, "Thief!"

"Yes, you'll see the birds again," Alika assured him.

Sulu kept talking about the birds for a long time, until his small voice faded out. He was different from all the other boys in Nunatak, Alika knew, a carver and bird lover.

Alika had his own memories of the springs and summers onshore. They paraded through his mind after Sulu had gone to sleep.

He remembered riding, as a child, on the sledge as the dogs drew it across the new grass of May. He remembered gathering bird eggs toward the end of the summer, when he was not much higher than Jamka.

He remembered picking heather to line the caribou-hide sleeping mattresses for the sealskin tents in which they slept. He remembered gathering cotton flowers for use with dried moss to make wicks for the seal-oil lamps. He remembered picking crowberries and blueberries and cranberries to be dried for Mama's winter cooking. Red bearberries ripened in the fall.

Most of all, he remembered going hunting for the first time with his papa for musk oxen and caribou and wolves and hares. Hares were hunted by the thousands, as much for their skin, which would be made into socks, as for their meat. Eider ducks were snared.

Fishing for Arctic char, food for man and dog, began in the spring through lake and river ice. In the fall, the ice was sometimes so transparent the fish could be seen swimming beneath Alika's boots.

During the spring and summer hunting, fishing, and food gathering, Alika's family often met friends and neighbors from Nunatak, sharing food and talk and songs, sometimes throat singing. Standing face-to-face, they'd make a sound in their throats without opening their mouths. The sounds were inspired by those of the birds or other animals. Mama was very good at it.

The shared food cooked by the women always tasted better than the food of winter. It could be smelled a mile away as the hunters returned to the campsites. The men occasionally did something special, like placing hot rocks in caribou stomachs filled with blood, to make an instant pudding. Alika loved that.

Beginning in May, the musk oxen shed large parts of their underfur, and it was gathered to be woven by the women. Almost everything on the tundra—animals, birds, and plants—was gathered. The migratory birds would begin to arrive, pleasing Sulu. And seal pups would be born out on the strait.

Alika clearly remembered summers when the wolves got to a herd of musk oxen before the hunters. The musk oxen formed a circle, with the cows inside, and the wolves attacked. The bulls on the outside of the circle rammed the wolves as best they could, and the hunters shot the wolves and then the musk oxen.

Thinking about those days, from the time of childhood until the past spring and summer, Alika felt desolate and sad, lonelier than ever.

He reached across Jamka's belly to put his hand on his brother's shoulder. Sulu stirred but did not awaken. Alika soon went to uneasy sleep.

The floes, common in the Greenland Strait during

the long winters, were sometimes occupied by seal hunters,

going out in their kayaks, risking high winds

and blizzards.

13

In the first week of the *kabloonas'* January, the moon was very near the horizon, so it was not much assistance to Alika's hunting. Two days later, Jamka found three possible seal holes, but it was too cold for Alika to sit at them. Sulu stayed home.

Alika took the carbine with him, of course. But he shook with cold and could not hold the rifle steady. His fingers were numb despite his mitts. He would not have been able to pull the trigger should a bear have appeared.

Every day they'd go outside for a few minutes to stand in the blackness and look at the *iglu,* seeing the warm light of the *qulliq* through the nearly transparent blocks of snow. It seemed to be the only light in a planet of ebony.

On the tenth morning of January, a towering berg slammed into the stern of their ice ship, shaking it, pushing from behind, and then finally spinning away in the wind and the currents.

Watching it go, Sulu asked, "What else can happen to us?"

Alika forced a laugh. "Not much. A berg knocked us loose from shore. A bear stole our food. We almost got lost in a blizzard. We got frostbitten. What did I miss?"

"We've been missing the feast every week!"

"I hadn't thought about that," Alika said.

"I have. Everybody is in the meeting hall, eating and laughing and singing."

Alika said quietly, "Those are good things to think about. It won't be too long until we're there with everyone again."

Alika didn't want to talk about the future, when the floe would come apart, though it certainly would happen. But not a day or night went by that he didn't think about it.

By mid-January, the moon was full again, and Alika and Jamka were out hunting. Sulu huddled a few feet away, staying near his big brother. The moon was shining so brightly that they could see miles ahead. Mock moons were on either side of it.

Without warning, Jamka tensed. His tail rose straight up, front legs rigid.

Alika held his breath and slowly raised the harpoon. The indicator rod trembled, and the nose of a seal plugged the breathing hole as Alika drove the harpoon head into it, Jamka howling and Sulu yelling, "We can eat! We can eat!"

Alika yelled triumphantly, "Yes, we can!"

The animal was fat, and Alika dressed it in the main *iglu,* having learned his lesson about storage in the small house and guarding their meals from *nanuk.*

The crosscurrents began playing tricks in the afternoon, steering the floe westward, then eastward. It was a ship without a rudder.

"What's happening?" Sulu asked, face showing alarm.

"I don't know. Every day we go farther south and there's nothing we can do about it," Alika answered. No one really understood the waters in the strait and how they changed night and day. "Let's just hope the currents push us toward shore."

Early the next afternoon, when they were down at the floe edge with Jamka intently watching a hole, Sulu yelled, *"Nanuk!"* and Alika turned around, grabbing the Maynard.

Thirty feet away, coming in their direction, was one of the largest bears Alika had ever seen. Jamka leaped away from the seal hole, and the bear headed in a run for the Little One, about ten feet away.

Alika heard the bear puff and fired, hitting it in the head, blood spurting as it hurtled down the short slope, plunging into the water.

Sulu had dropped into the snow face-first, and Alika sank down, shaking all over.

Jamka appeared puzzled as he watched the *nanuk* beginning to float away, leaving a red streak behind. It had all happened so quickly that none of them could move. The bear would have provided at least three months of food. Old Miak had lived on bear meat his last four months.

Finally, Alika said, "It was bound to happen." He went over and sat beside his brother, an arm around Sulu's small shoulders. "Papa warned that the bear would make a puff before it attacked. I pulled the trigger when I heard the puff."

"It is probably the same bear that came here before, the one that broke into the storage *iglu*. It knew we were here," Alika said.

"And he could have eaten all of us," Sulu said, still breathing hard.

That was true, Alika thought. Bears ate seals; wolves ate caribou and musk oxen; foxes ate lemmings and hares, and dined on the leavings of bears, quarreling with ravens over which got the last bites. Bears also ate unlucky humans. And humans ate all of the animals.

Looking at the bear floating away, the blood running down over its black nose and spreading, Alika felt sorry for it. He'd never really liked to look at the five *nanuk* skulls in his front yard, although he knew it was tradition to save them, and he knew all hunters had great respect for the beautiful bears and their spirits. He also believed there was indeed a place where bears lived somewhere in the sky. Inu said he'd been there, and Alika believed him.

Alika had never thought he would have to kill one. But his family had slept on bearskins for years, and they all wore bearskin pants. Bears had been good to them.

He had watched, and even helped, as his papa and mama had cut up the carcasses of bears, rejoicing that they'd have the meat and hides. Yet they expressed sorrow each time that such a beautiful animal had to die.

The third week in January, the sun came out weakly after mostly hiding for more than eighty days. Alika and Sulu celebrated by shouting, "Sikrinaktok! The sun shines!" and hugging each other. The terrible darkness was almost over.

Sulu shouted, "Oh, how I wish I was home!"

There would be the annual feasts, and children would go from dwelling to dwelling, snuffing out the old moss wicks in the *qulliqs* and inserting new wicks, lighting them with stones and flints. Everyone would eat until his or her belly couldn't hold another morsel.

The children would be singing or shouting:

"The welcome sun returns!
 Amna ajah, ah-huh,
 And brings us weather fine and fair,
 Amna ajah, ah-hu."

The next day, Sulu finished his raven carving. It was ten inches tall. He blackened it with burnt wick moss from the *qulliq*.

"It's beautiful," said Alika.

"I'll give it to Inu," Sulu said proudly.

Alika said, "Brother, you're a master carver already."

Sulu had used the sharp steel knife from the *Reliance* to make the rough-looking throat feathers, the wedge-shaped tail, and the thin but sturdy legs. The replica looked exactly like Punna.

It was the month of Alika's fifteenth birthday, and he celebrated by making *aalu*. Missing was a bit of ptarmigan intestine. There was no substitute for the bird on the floe. Sulu said the sauce tasted better without it.

A single bowhead whale could provide Nunatak
with more fuel for cooking, heating, and lighting than
a thousand seals. But the bowheads seldom came
anywhere near the village.

14

Kussu and Maja had watched the weak return of the sun, and Maja said to herself, "I have to go now. I must!" The sun would become stronger each day. Then she said to her husband, "I've got to find them." She'd constantly talked about going south ever since their boys had disappeared.

"I forbid it," Kussu replied. He had broken his leg on a recent caribou hunt and couldn't go.

For more than three months, they had both agonized over their missing sons, each in his or her own way. There had been days and nights of the terrible darkness when they hardly spoke. They'd repeatedly prayed to the spirits. But what had happened—or what was happening—to Alika and Sulu was a torment that could not be relieved by Inu or any of their neighbors.

And Maja had talked endlessly to old Miak, asking him to try to remember each day of life on his floe, each night. In particular she wanted to know when the floe began to break up and where he had been rescued by hunters in their kayaks.

"We must wait until my leg is better," said Kussu firmly. He still hobbled around on a homemade crutch. "We must go together." He had made the family a new sledge.

"No, I cannot wait for you, and you can't ride the sledge, Kussu. You'll tire the dogs," Maja said. She'd made up her mind. Nothing would stop her from going.

"Do you know what you're doing?" Kussu asked angrily. "Do you have any idea how far you have to go?"

"Yes, Miak told me where he was rescued. It was off a village called Tarjuaq."

"And if you don't find them at sea off that village, what do you do?"

"Miak told me the next one down is Angijuak."

"Maja, this is crazy. You'll go hundreds and hundreds of miles by yourself."

"I'll have the dogs. I'll hunt along the way. Kussu, it's the only chance we have before the ice across all the inlets and rivers breaks up. I'll have to cross all of them by sledge. I don't know the ice as well as you do, but I know I can do it."

Kussu shook his head in despair. There were dozens of inlets, bays, and rivers all the way to the end of Baffin Island and Hudson Bay. She would never find the boys. She might die.

But Maja had thought about this trip for weeks, well before the sun crept out. She'd even asked ancient Aninga, who could no longer hunt and relied on the good graces of his neighbors for food and seal oil, if she could borrow his rifle and some bullets.

She said, "Husband, make sure I have everything I'll need for the trip. I want enough meat to last the first two weeks. I can kill seals as well as you can. I'll stop in any villages along the way to rest and resupply. I'll need your harpoon. Aninga is lending me his rifle."

Kussu again shook his head. "There will be gales and driving snow. We know only two villages that are south of here."

"Salluk and Anami."

Kussu gave up talking about it. But a moment later, he said, "What about the dogs? You won't have Jamka to lead them."

"Nattiq and I get along just fine. He isn't as strong as Jamka, but he has the strength I need. He's a good lead dog."

Most important, she thought, the dogs could run without food for nearly a week and still pull the load.

Kussu gave up, still angry that his wife wouldn't listen. He'd make sure the sledge had everything she would need. Food, seal oil for the soapstone lamp, a harpoon, knives, caribou robes, and a sleeping bag. Plus a half dozen other survival items.

But he did, in a last effort, ask the hunters to come by and discourage her from even trying to reach Baffin Island, which would likely be near the end of her mission. One hunter, Shukok, asked, "Suppose you are crossing one of the inlets and the ice gives way?"

Maja looked straight at Shukok and replied, "Along with the dogs I will die."

None of the hunters volunteered to go with her. Kussu had asked them not to, hoping she'd change her mind.

She gathered the women of the village into the community hall and told them of her plans. Most of them, especially those who had children, understood why she was willing to give her life to rescue her sons. She asked them to help her by making booties out of sealskin for the dogs.

Kussu said, "Even with the booties, you'll have to stop and check their paws often. You know the ice can cut. You have to spread the toes apart and look for trouble."

Maja had grown up with dogs, winters and summers, and knew all about how to care for them, but she let her husband advise her, trying to make him a part of what had to be done. She knew that he, the brave hunter, loving father, family protector, was torn apart inside that she'd be on a journey no man had ever tried. Just the idea wounded his pride. So he had to give advice about things she already knew.

"I'll check their paws every hour," she promised.

Facing the inevitable, Kussu had been groaning and sighing for three days, with spurts of anger between, knowing that his wife could not be stopped. He'd even enlisted Inu to make her change her mind, but the shaman said, "Let her go! She'll return."

"When will I see you again?" Kussu asked Maja one evening.

She answered, "After the winter freeze makes the ice safe. Our sons will be with me." Ten months perhaps.

Five days later, with six hundred booties for use in late spring when the ice began to melt and a fourteen-day supply of frozen raw seal meat to be shared with the dogs, noon sun shining above, moon fortunately due up that night, Maja shouted to Nattiq, *"Huk! Huk! Huk!"* And off she went, the women of Nunatak cheering her. The eight Greenland huskies were straining to go, howling loudly.

Kussu, standing outside their dwelling, had tears in his eyes. He might never see his wife again.

The nine-foot sledge used a typical fan hitch. The dogs were attached to the sledge with individual long sealskin ropes called traces. Their harnesses were made of sealskin. Short lines were attached with toggles made of walrus ivory, fitting into a loop at the end of a long rope of walrus skin, hooked to a short line of walrus from the front of the sledge with a connector also made of walrus ivory. The brake was a long, braided sealskin line looped several times and thrown forward over the front end of one of the runners to create friction and stop the sledge.

The wooden runners were coated with frozen char, bound with seal rope, and when she was not running behind the sledge, Maja would ride it, holding on to the wooden crossbar. Her long, braided whip of sealskin was used to guide the dogs, not lash them.

The village of Salluk was forty miles south, and Maja thought she could make at least four miles an hour running along the shore and crossing the frozen inlets, skirting around any piles of drift ice. If the dogs got tangled, which they certainly would, she'd have to stop and untangle them. That was routine. She'd done it even when pregnant with Alika and Sulu. She planned to be in Salluk late the next afternoon, running all night by moonlight.

She knew what she faced—wilderness and perhaps bitter wind with spikes of snow driven before it She'd wear a snow-and-wind mask made of walrus hide when necessary. By the coast, there'd be no trees. Those were all inland, in the mountains, far west across the tundra. There'd be silence except for the whisper of the sledge runners. The dogs would not break the silence unless they saw a *nanuk*—then they'd roar.

She likely would not come across a single human. Maybe a blue or white fox, maybe a bear. She would fight loneliness in this world of white. She would force herself to think only of Alika and Sulu.

The sea doesn't freeze solid to the ocean floor because the downward growth of the floating masses is stopped when the ice itself acts as a blanket to prevent the water from losing its natural heat.

15

It was early February. Alika and Sulu watched as the aurora borealis streamers, in twilight, moved from west to east, forming a curtain of yellow and white. That was the general color except in the northwest, where the sky was deep red.

Sulu said, "I'm still afraid of those lights."

"They haven't harmed us, have they?" Alika pointed out. More icebergs were in view, a threatening fleet of them. "I'm more worried about the bergs than the sky."

The next day, twilight lasted from dawn until late afternoon, another good sign that light was returning. But then a heavy snowfall and high winds began in the early evening. The three of them again stayed inside. It was typical High Arctic weather in late winter. No two days or nights alike. It could change on the hour.

For almost four months, Alika had been trying to guide the conversation away from home, but Sulu persisted almost every day and night, often asking the very same questions. Alika always tried to answer them without repeating himself.

"You think that Papa and Mama have forgotten us?"

"No, they have not." But Alika knew that they might, by now, have some doubts that their sons were still alive.

"How about the dogs? Have they forgotten us?"

"Not at all. They'll jump all over us once we come home," Alika said.

"How about Inu?"

"No. He'd never forget us. Shamans never forget anything."

Alika's mind was more on the snowhouse than on Sulu's questions. He'd built the original *iglus* not far from the west edge of the floe, and already there were signs of crumbling the farther south it sailed. The sun would warm the water. Melting was inevitable. Or those miserable crosscurrents could suddenly cause a split exactly underneath their house. It might happen in the middle of the night, leaving them a narrow wedge of ice on which to scramble. There'd likely be no warning. Alika decided to build another snowhouse nearer the middle of the floe the next day.

"What is Mama making for dinner tonight?" Sulu asked.

Without thinking, Alika said, "Oh, maybe caribou stew with those dried blackberries," and then regretted it. He also longed for the warmth and protection of their home, and meals his mama prepared. He also longed for safety. That might be a matter of luck.

Sulu asked, "Will we ever see them again?"

"Of course we will. Now go to sleep."

When they went outside in the morning, they saw fresh *nanuk* tracks in the new white snow cover.

Jamka sniffed them and Sulu said, "Another bear swam out."

"Looks that way," Alika said in a calm voice. "Don't wander around." He had already reloaded the Maynard.

They built the new snowhouse that morning and

moved their meager possessions. It was near the middle of the floe, where the ice was thickest. It would be the last section to peel off. Alika moved what was left of the sledge. It was now a matter of waiting.

The next day, there were beautiful crimson clouds to the south, a sign of spring, and Alika killed and dressed another medium-sized seal. "Our luck has changed, you see," he said to Sulu.

The following day, the tops of the southern Greenland mountains were briefly illuminated by the sun and many narwhals swam around, their tusks sometimes projecting over the pack ice.

"That's not good. They scare the seals away," Alika said.

"I remember Papa saying that," Sulu said.

Kussu had begun teaching Sulu about hunting when he was four or five, but Sulu didn't seem very interested. There was no school in Nunatak for the children. Hunting would be what their lives were all about. By the time he was twelve, Alika had gone to the ice by himself to hunt. That was his proud destiny, like his papa's.

"Two more years, when you're twelve, you can go anywhere by yourself," Alika said.

Let his brother think about what was ahead in

his life, Alika decided. Let him think about being brave and strong. Let him know how great it would be for all in the village to call him hunter.

The light was changing rapidly. The moon was not quite full, but the light was so strong by midday that even the stars couldn't be seen. Alika said to Sulu, "The sun and the moon are competing to give us light."

One morning Alika and Sulu were watching the light increase on the southern horizon. In not too long a time, the whole orb appeared and stayed above the horizon for a short while, a red ball over the strait to the southwest.

"Every day it will get stronger," Alika said.

Always curious, Sulu asked, "Who makes the light?"

"The sun does, and when the sun disappears, we have dark. You know that."

"Yes, but is there a shaman up in the sky who makes it happen?"

"I don't think so," Alika replied.

"Someone does it," Sulu said.

Alika said, "You ask me questions I can't answer. Ask Papa and Mama when we get home. If they can't answer you, talk to Inu."

"Suppose he doesn't know."

Alika shook his head, saying, "Little One, you're driving me crazy."

In the afternoon, Alika harpooned a seal and butchered it immediately.

Floe ice covers all the surfaces of the bays, inlets, and straits of the Arctic coast during the winter. It is usually strong enough to carry hunters and sledges.

16

Maja stayed two days in Salluk, a village of sixty sod-and-stone huts, sitting out a gale. Lodging with a family of four, she fretted about the time lost. The people had welcomed her, amazed at what she was trying to do.

When she rode into Salluk, there had been a short vicious fight, a tangle not unexpected, between her dogs and the local ones. The fight was Nattiq's fault. He picked it. Maja and the Salluk hunters broke it up. Everyone in the Arctic knew about dog-fights. They could be bloody and could end in death. Fighting and toughness were part of sledge-dog life.

The run between Nunatak and Salluk had been uneventful. Nattiq and the team had pulled well, even joyfully. The dogs always preferred to run, day or night, rather than burrow down in the snow to sleep. Their muscles worked as though they were encased in seal oil. Inuit believed huskies were put on Earth precisely to do this work.

The first night, the villagers had crowded into the largest hut to hear Maja's story about Alika and Sulu. They also wanted to learn what was occurring in the larger Nunatak, a settlement they envied. They'd heard about the wrecked *Reliance* and what gifts of wood and other materials it had bestowed. They were jealous.

Villagers in the High Arctic were always curious about any visitor. A visitor could be talked about for winters to come, especially a rarity like Maja, the mother determined to rescue her sons no matter the odds, no matter how dangerous.

"My name is Maja, and I'm the wife of hunter Kussu, who has a broken leg. I was born in Nunatak. My mother died of high fever when I was six; my father was drowned in the strait when I was fourteen," Maja said.

She spoke in a matter-of-fact voice and further told them what she and Kussu thought had happened to Alika and Sulu. No questions were asked. This was the Arctic. What was there to say?

A black-bearded hunter rose and spoke. "Turn back, woman," he said.

Maja simply looked at him and the conversation was over.

When she left the hut, he stepped out of the shadows. "I've been south," he said. "Watch out for snow-covered rocks when you are near the shore. If you break a runner and have no hunter to fix it, you may have to walk a long way to the next settlement."

She thanked him for his good advice, then said, "I've broken a runner before and fixed it myself."

"Do you want me to come with you to Anami?"

Anami was the next village to the south, four sleeps away.

Maja thanked the hunter again but said she didn't want to interrupt his life. She had an idea he had no wife or children. There weren't too many single men in the Arctic. They always needed female companionship—women to cook, make their clothing, and have their children.

He said, "Be careful of whirlpools when you cross the river inlets."

Leftovers of the summer torrents, whirlpools were frozen but the ice was often dangerously weak. It was almost impossible to know where they were, and Nattiq, out ahead of the sledge, had probably never led a team across a frozen river. Dogs and driver could plunge into the brackish water beneath the ice hole in an instant and die.

"And watch out for the wind," he said.

She knew about the wind simply from growing up in Nunatak, having been blown off her feet in past winters. "I will," she said.

"*Nanuk.*"

She nodded.

"Frostbite!"

Maja's cheeks and nose had been frostbitten when she was in her teens, but the injury to her skin had been minor.

She nodded again. "Thank you."

He said, "Good luck," and faded back into the shadows.

Maja slept soundly, and in the early morning twilight, she thanked the family for housing her, awakened the dogs, and made certain their pulling traces were in good shape and clear of tangles. She mounted the sledge and yelled, "*Huk! Huk! Huk!*" in response to the dogs' loud howls—and was off to Anami.

Just as there had been no trail from Nunatak to

Salluk, only animal-tracked snow and ice, there was no trail to Anami. She hoped that there'd be *inuksuk,* piles of guiding rocks sometimes resembling humans. These were usually built to mark routes along the coast. She hoped there would be no cloud cover to hide the sun, and no gales to blow and force her to stop during the next twenty hours.

Halfway to Anami, Maja fed the dogs, and herself, with seal meat from home, then rested them. The dogs burrowed down in the snow, and Maja lay down on the sledge. It was past midnight. The sky was clear, and a three-quarter moon was out. The run so far had again been without event. It had been so easy that her hidden doubts and fears had almost vanished. She was awake for a while, thinking of the boys, then of Kussu.

Over the past tortured months, she'd made herself imagine Alika as a fully grown experienced hunter, not the squealing red seal that had come from between her legs, not the always hungry *atertok* she'd nursed for two years, but a man now almost as capable as Kussu. She'd pictured him moving around on the floe doing everything that an adult hunter should do, as well as taking care of Sulu.

Looking at the moon in the windless silence so

deep that it seemed a falling snowflake would make a noise, she thought of her husband, thought again of the bitter words they'd had just before she'd departed, wounding words they'd never before said to each other. She realized again she was destroying his pride as a man, a hunter. No matter what happened on her search, however long it took before she returned to Nunatak, she knew that their marriage might never recover. She had done the worst thing that could be done to any man, and Kussu was, above all, a *piosuriyok,* a brave man in every muscle of his body. She loved him dearly. With their two boys in hand, she'd beg for forgiveness when they met again.

Maja also knew he might divorce her during her year's absence from their bed. The ceremony was traditional. She would lie on her back in the sleeping space of a good friend, her knees drawn up, a cord around her head. Kisanqua, a close neighbor, would stand over her, holding the cord in her hands, uttering a chant, frequently changing the tone and measure, at intervals pulling the cord and raising Maja's head. The ritual, which Kussu could not attend, would continue for two hours, blaming

Maja. Then she would be divorced but could hope to remarry Kussu at a later date.

She willed herself to sleep.

It was nearing dawn when she awakened, and the calm weather hadn't changed. She relieved herself, ate some snow, and woke up Nattiq and the dogs from their burrowed warmth. Less than one sleep to Anami—another easy run.

The Arctic coast is actually warmer than many places to the south during winter. The record low is sixty-three degrees below zero. Although the windblown snowdrifts can be twenty feet deep, the usual ground cover is only a few inches. Wind is the deciding factor.

17

Midweek in early March, with days and nights of equal length, Alika was unhappily watching a seal hole on the west edge of the floe, hundreds of feet from the snowhouse. Sulu and Jamka were perched beside him. The day before, the sun had stayed out until three o'clock, bringing good spirits. One huge, scary berg had come so close that it made a dark shadow on the floe, but it did not hit them.

Two days before, there had been another high wind, keeping them inside, sweeping the snow off the ice, leaving a glassy surface. And the previous night had been terrifying. They'd again listened to the cracking, splitting, and groaning noises of the ice and the hollow sounds of rolling chunks of it beneath the floe. Alika had tried to calm Sulu, but he, too, had been anxious. Alika believed it was only a matter of a week or two until their floe would break up into pieces of free-floating ice.

Although the sun was now dimly out most of the day, the cold was penetrating, and Sulu said, "I'm going back to the house."

Standing up he lost his balance, flailing his arms and sliding down the ice into the water, letting out a panic-laden scream, hitting the back of his head against the hard crust.

Jamka dove in behind him, grabbing him by the parka hood, keeping him from floating away. He treaded water as Sulu yelled, "Help us, Alika!"

It was all Alika could do to keep from also sliding in on his knees as he grasped Jamka's harness. The dog helped with his front paws, hooking them over the ice.

Sulu was rasping from shock, water seeping through the narrow space between his throat and the parka collar. His mouth was wide open as he tried to catch his breath.

"We'll get you out!" Alika shouted.

Straining to tug both his brother and Jamka up over the rim, Alika shouted, "Help us, Sulu!"

But Sulu's brown face was already turning white, and his eyes had enlarged like those of a caribou about to be attacked by wolves. Paralyzed, the Little One couldn't help.

It took the strength of both Alika and Jamka to pull him out of the water and up onto the floe surface. Alika's heart was hammering, and Jamka shook himself, letting the droplets fly.

They dragged the dripping Sulu to the house, leaving a water streak in the snow behind them, finally pulling him through the entry tunnel. He was breathing heavily and shivering, murmuring, "Oh, oh, oh."

Alika quickly stripped him naked and piled the caribou sleeping-robes on top of him, then started a fire in the *qulliq*. He had Sulu sip some warm water.

"We'll get you dry and warm, Little One."

Alika remembered how his mama had dried and warmed him after he'd fallen through lake ice and had been rescued by Jamka. She'd used a *Reliance* towel, then tucked him into his sleeping bag. She'd rubbed Jamka dry, too, and put his warm body against Alika's.

He would do the same for Sulu. Then he'd rub Jamka dry with a polar-bear square and insert him into Sulu's sleeping bag. After that was accomplished, he'd begin to dry Sulu's clothes over the *qulliq* flame.

But it would not be as easy in the snowhouse as it had been in the timber-and-sod house in Nunatak. Almost all the hunters had fallen into sea or lake water at one time or another. None knew how to swim or had any desire to learn. Water was as hostile as a *nanuk*. The hunters knew what to do when they took a plunge, but some died.

Teeth chattering, Sulu shivered for more than an hour nestled against Jamka. The dog, seeming to know what his role was—arctic dogs had furnished body heat over many centuries—mostly slept. But Sulu's drawn face still hadn't returned to its brown color.

Alika had quickly made a wooden drying rack out of odd sledge pieces for Sulu's clothing. It would take several days before his brother could dress again, though. The low flame from the cotton-grass wick was steady but not all that hot.

There was enough oil in the walrus bladders to last perhaps a week if they used it sparingly. But Alika knew he'd have to kill a seal within several days, and that meant leaving Sulu alone. Jamka would be needed to find a promising hole quickly.

Sitting on the sleeping ledge beside Sulu, Alika said, "Little One, I have to hunt tomorrow."

"And leave me alone?" Sulu's face showed alarm.

"We won't be that far away."

"Leave Jamka with me."

"No, I need Jamka to do his job."

"Then wait until my clothes are dry."

"I can't, Little One. We need oil and meat every day. You know that."

Sulu didn't answer, turning his head toward the snow-block wall.

Alika knew how quiet, lonely, and shadow-dark the cold snowhouse could be. Once, long ago on a hunt with his papa, he'd gotten sick and had to stay alone in their tiny *iglu* for two days. He'd watched the flickering blue light of the *qulliq* for hours, between sleeps. He remembered his fear of being without a rifle or even a harpoon. What if *nanuk* had smelled him inside there and broken through the blocks?

Weeping softly, and without turning around, Sulu asked the same question he'd asked for months, "Brother, when will this be over?"

Alika had only one answer: "Soon, I hope."

"You keep saying that."

One thing was certain: Before long, their ship of ice would crumble into thousands of pieces, and Alika would need to find one large enough to carry

Sulu, Jamka, and himself. If Nuliajuk was indeed looking up from the bottom of the sea, the floe would shatter in the daylight, not at night. Alika had never seen a floe come apart but could imagine the ice splitting in large pieces, one after another, then the large pieces shattering into smaller ones; frightening noises; and then, at last, the shock of being dumped into the water. Alika planned to make a paddle from sledge parts and try to reach shore when that happened. He'd long ago given up thoughts of rescue.

Free-floating pack ice can be wide expanses of flat chunks or terrifying towers, tumbled blocks, pushed about by winds or currents. During high winds, the pieces can make explosive noises crashing against one another.

18

The gale from the west, driving snow ahead of it, struck Maja when she was near Anami. She got on the lee side of the sledge, huddling with the dogs. Her face was freezing beneath her mask. She was exhausted from trying to control the team. Fights had broken out, and she came near using the rifle on the biggest husky, which had challenged Nattiq for leadership.

The going had been slow in the gale, and Maja, at one point when the dogs were almost totally out of control, flailed them with the whip, weeping shamelessly. Maybe Kussu had been right. She was not strong enough to make this trip alone, though she would never admit that to anyone. Her legs and back ached.

The early March wind roared, and the snow curled over the side of the sledge. Maja's mittened hands pulled the parka hood tighter against her throat; her body was lodged between two dogs, one of them the husky she'd wanted to shoot. She'd felt lonely before while solo trapping on the tundra but never this lonely, this defeated. She finally fell asleep in her caribou bag.

When Maja awakened, she was warm; the curling snow had covered her and the dogs completely. The sun was up and the morning was brilliant. Rested, she felt better, and if the dogs would cooperate, she might make Anami by darkness.

She fed them, and while they ate, she wondered, as she did each day, where the boys were. Just how far south had they drifted down the strait? She steadfastly believed they were still alive.

They are my boys. No man could understand the strength of bond between a mother and her children. She'd given life to Alika and Sulu in a separate shelter, an *iynivik,* and she'd cut their umbilical cords with a piece of flint. She'd named both of them after recently deceased uncles, both hunters. She'd placed the cords in a pouch in her parka. Then she had settled in an *iglu,* built by Kussu, for three weeks, a time during which women were considered impure and dangerous because of giving birth. The custom was ages old.

Alika and Sulu were her boys, and Maja willed them to live, absolutely willed them to live on their floe. *They must defy death.*

Soon she hooked up the dog traces and got under way for Anami. The running was smooth for the next hour, but suddenly there was a muffled sound and the sledge careened on its side, throwing Maja off, causing the dogs to tangle. She knew immediately what had happened. She'd hit an unseen rock. Getting to her feet, she saw that the left runner was torn away from the sledge.

There was a coil of seal rope that Kussu had attached to the frame, but the frozen runner had broken into a half dozen lengths on impact and there was no way to tie them together. She'd have to wait until she got to Anami and see if a villager there would give her a piece of wood or whalebone for a replacement.

Maja would have more difficulty controlling the dogs now that they couldn't run. Fights would break out more easily. The sledge would drag slowly at an angle, and keeping the dogs in fan position would be difficult. She'd walk behind the broken sledge. She'd use the whip and take a piece of ear out of any dog that misbehaved. She had to challenge the dogs, each of them stronger than she was.

The dogs spotted the *nanuk* before Maja saw it, and they jerked the tracer line out of her hands, dragging the tumbling sledge with the rifle still attached to it. Maja could only stand and watch as the roaring pack attacked the bear, the pull tracers entangling it.

She saw the bear's paw strike Nattiq as he led the attack, knocking the dog aside in a flurry of blood. It was the wildest dog-bear fight she'd ever seen. The eight dogs sank their teeth into the enraged bear's back and belly. She ran forward and wrested the rifle off the sledge frame, moving toward the melee to get a clean shot at the *nanuk*.

She got close to the bear, which was still upright, with the dogs tearing at his flesh, and took aim at his head. She fired at an ear and the bear toppled over. Maja collapsed in the bloodred snow, weak-kneed from fright. On her back, panting in terror, she watched as the dogs, muttering and growling, ripped through the bear's thick coat to get at his hot meat. Her heart pounded.

They ate as savagely as they had fought, and Maja made no attempt to stop them. When they'd had their fill, she took her *ulu* and cut a chunk of meat for herself, her face getting bloody from the goodness of the bear. Then she untangled the traces and dragged the carcass to the sledge, strapping it to the frame for the villagers of Anami.

After the delay, she was under way again, hoping to reach the village without further trouble.

As the moon shone down, Maja arrived safely in Anami just before midnight. The village dogs set up a din and awakened everyone. Anami was smaller than Salluk, only forty families living there. Most came out because visitors were few and far between at any time of day. The villagers welcomed the woman who brought the gift of a bear carcass.

What men were there and not out hunting took care of the dogs, and Maja soon went to sleep in the house of Kuukittsaq.

In the morning, after she told them of her search,

the oldest and most traveled hunter, Aku, shook his head and said, "Woman, do you want to die and never see your children again?"

Maja answered steadily, "I am capable of going south." There was defiance in her voice. She was tired of men trying to tell her what to do.

His laugh was harsh. "Even I wouldn't try it. There are no settlements below here for hundreds of sleeps. I've traveled south for days, and there is nothing but foxes and wolves and bears and snow and bad ice. No people."

Maja said, "I must go on."

Aku, whose face was tattooed like a woman's, thin black lines around his cheeks and chin, said, "There are inlets and rivers that are frozen now, but soon the ice will begin to melt and you will risk your life trying to cross them. And shortly after that, the river water will be rushing out to sea. Woman, there is no safe traveling between here and the end of Ellesmere. The inlets are like *nanuk* teeth."

Maja said, "I must go on," but her voice was wavering and weakening.

"Woman, if your sons are still alive, they will get off the floe and get ashore without your help. Go back to Nunatak. I will fix your sledge. Go home, foolish woman, still alive."

For two days, Maja thought about what Aku had said, knowing that he spoke the truth. For two sleepless nights, she rolled back and forth in her caribou bag. During the day, she talked to Kuukittsaq, who had two children. For every hour that she was defiant of the elements, she spent another hour thinking. They talked about what could happen during the hundreds of sleeps to the end of Ellesmere; then the crossing to what the *kabloonas* called Devon; and below that the place called Baffin Island, where Miak had been rescued. Kuukittsaq said, "Don't go."

Finally, Maja gave up and decided to return home. The men of the village had already fixed her sledge. At least she had tried, and if she ever saw Alika and Sulu again, she could tell them about her short journey and why she had turned back. She hoped they'd understand, but she remained angry at herself—and at the bearded hunter at Salluk and this man with the tattooed face, both of whom had robbed her with their warning words, played on her unspoken fear.

She arrived back at Nunatak in four sleeps,

barely stopping to eat, pushing Nattiq and his team like they'd never been driven before. Defeat rode with her every mile.

She fell into Kussu's arms and said, "I failed; I'm sorry…" They wept together, and an exhausted Maja soon went to sleep. She'd wait until the next day to tell him what had happened.

There could be thousands of small ice floes in the strait,

bobbing up and down, rubbing against one another

in round shapes or triangles or uneven squares.

They often freeze together, forming a new surface

as rough as newly plowed earth.

19

Frustrated, Alika returned home from the seal holes empty-handed after another all-day watch. The ones that Jamka had chosen had not delivered a single shiny head. He estimated they had enough food for seven days.

Sulu had begun to wheeze and cough, the certain delayed result of falling into the water. Alika felt his forehead. It was hot and feverish, and Sulu's eyes were watery. He had awakened that morning saying he didn't feel well. "I'm sick, Alika. I hurt all over."

"I'll fix you some tea," Alika said. He had no other remedy.

Papa had put some leaves from the wild-growing Labrador plant on the sledge. The leaves had been plucked from the summer tundra. The hot tea had been used for hundreds of winters as a curing drink. Shamans did the best they could with herbs.

"It's no time for you to get sick, Sulu."

"I know."

Alika was as healthy as a young musk ox. The cold weather kept most Inuit healthy. He could remember being sick only that one time when they'd been hunting, but he could remember many days when his little brother had to stay inside on the platform.

Alika boiled water for the tea and fixed supper. "You have to eat something," he said.

Sulu wasn't interested in eating. Restless, he coughed all night.

In the morning, Alika was frightened when he discovered his brother had an even higher fever. His forehead was burning. Beyond giving him more tea, Alika had no idea how to treat him. He did remember that the one time Sulu had had a high fever, Mama had kept putting ice-cold towels on his forehead and throat. The cold had seemed to bring the fever down

He went outside to chop ice, then used a bearskin square to apply it. Sulu still coughed and was breathing heavily.

Alika said, with useless anger, "Don't do this to me, Sulu. Please don't. You have to get well."

"I will," Sulu promised, with closed eyes.

Just the idea of the Little One dying on this inhuman floe was unthinkable. But Alika knew fever. It could kill. It did kill.

Alika stayed by the sleeping platform all day, talking to Sulu about everything he could think of—home and their parents, Inu and the people of the village. Sulu remained silent, falling asleep, awakening, reaching for Alika's hand whenever it applied the cold compress.

At one point, Sulu awoke and said, "I wish Mama was here."

"So do I," Alika replied. "She'd know exactly what to do."

"Yes, she would."

Another time, Sulu said, "There was a medicine man on the *Reliance;* Mama told me."

"Yes, but he had another name. He wasn't a shaman."

"Mama said that when all those white people

went south, the ship's medicine man gave Inu a lot of cure things, but Inu threw them into the water. Why did he do that?"

"Inu was afraid they might make us sick."

"Is Inu always right?" Sulu asked.

Alika hesitated. "I think so."

"Talk to him about me," Sulu said, and began coughing.

"I'll try to," Alika promised.

He looked up into the dome ceiling and said, "Inu, hello. This is me, Alika. Sulu is very sick and we need your help. He fell into the water four days ago, and now he has a bad fever. Tell me what to do. We're out here on a floe and can't get off. Talk to the spirits and tell us what to do . . ."

In late afternoon, Sulu, eyes reddened by the fever, was staring up at the dome of the snowhouse. He asked weakly, "Do you see the beautiful birds, Alika?"

Alika looked up through tears. "Yes." No birds were there, of course.

"The larks?"

"Yes."

"The snowy owls?"

"Um-huh."

"The loons and phalaropes?"

"Yes."

"The snow geese?"

"Yes."

"Do you hear them singing?"

"Yes."

"The raven? It goes, *Krrruack.*"

"Yes."

"The falcon? It goes, *Kek-kek.*"

"Yes, I know."

"The golden plovers? They have hoarse whistles. *Kweeee...*"

"Yes."

Then the weak voice stopped. Just stopped.

Sulu seemed to be giving up. He closed his eyes and Alika yelled angrily, "You can't die! You can't do this to me, leave me here alone!" He was suddenly enraged.

He slapped his brother hard on each cheek.

Sulu cried out painfully.

Alika yelled again. "Do not do this!"

Sulu's eyes were wide open, and he sobbed.

Anger and emotion quickly drained out of Alika,

and he sat on the platform beside Sulu, trying to think of what else to say. Finally, he said, "Please don't do that to me again. I'd want to die, too." Taking Sulu's hand, he said, "Get well, Little One. We're going home together. Soon!"

Slabs of glacier ice, calving off from shore, hit
the water with such impact that boats and even small
ships could be overturned by the huge waves.

20

Two days later, another gale roared in from the east, attacking the floe, causing nearby bergs to collide. The floe ice groaned, cracking and splitting around the edges, small and large pieces floating away to join the heaving surface of the strait. There was no snow or sleet, just savage wind. Listening to it, Alika guessed that the breakup was nearing. Then the wind abated, leaving a stiff, cold breeze, still from the east.

Alika knew the snowhouses would soon crumble, and the remains of the sledge that Papa had built would likely float into the North Atlantic. There'd be nothing left of the *Polar Star*.

A flock of noisy ducks appeared in the April sky, returning early from the south to spend the spring and summer above the Arctic Circle.

Sulu, his fever having subsided, said excitedly, "Look!"

Alika nodded. "Summer is on its way."

But the problem now was the breakup, and the danger of going into the freezing water and death. Even Jamka would not be able to swim ashore. Alika had cut a paddle from sledge wood.

He hoped that before he had to use the paddle, they'd be sighted by hunters. Yet there was no way to attract their attention beyond shouting, if they got close enough. He had no flag to wave, and the sound of the Maynard would die in the breeze. Another hope was that the east wind would continue to blow all day, taking the floe west, close to shore.

They hadn't eaten in almost two days. Alika simply hadn't been able to kill a seal. He was beginning to feel weak, so he got a length of seal rope from the small *iglu* to suck on, sharing it with Sulu and Jamka.

About noon, the sea began to wash across the floe, lapping aboard rather gently at first, then draining off as the floe undulated, the first sign of breakup. The inch-deep water wet their boots. Sulu was terrified, and Alika was almost as scared.

A lone raven winged overhead, flying toward land. Sulu didn't wave at it.

Swells began to rise about midnight, water splashing aboard, then draining off. Finally, Alika had to stand up, holding Sulu, too frightened to speak, on his shoulders. Jamka scrabbled for footing on the sledge. Three hours passed as they fought the sea. When the sun rose, the floe shattered into hundreds of chunks, some quite large and others the size of a caribou rump, some just slivers. The explosive sounds echoed throughout the Arctic dawn.

Carrying Sulu under one arm, the Punna carving stuffed into Sulu's parka, and holding the paddle in his free hand, Alika jumped aboard a raft of ice, followed by Jamka. Their new vessel was about five harpoons wide and ten long, perhaps a half harpoon deep. They were surrounded by a glassy sea of bobbing flat ice that stretched in each direction. Soon the sun was out strong, the whole peaceful world glittering.

On his knees, Alika paddled the ice raft toward shore. Sulu jabbered away, asking all sorts of questions that couldn't be answered. "Will we walk home?" They could see the coast.

There was still no wind, and the sky was clear, a perfect day. Jamka sat toward the bow, looking ahead, like a sailor on watch. Here and there, seals swam past. A whale surfaced on the port side, and the mist stayed in the air long after the bowhead descended to the depths. The water, between its patches of floating white, was blue-green.

A little later, in the distance, three kayaks, probably seal hunters, moved through the bobbing ice. Jamka spotted them first and howled.

Alika shook his head with massive relief, unable to believe that he was seeing humans again. It had been such a long time. His heart pounded. Were they real? Or was it some trick of the imagination? Hunters sometimes saw things that weren't there.

He took a chance and yelled, *"Hoy, hoy, hoy!"* And he kept yelling until they finally saw him.

Alika took some deep breaths. "We made it, Little One! We made it!"

Sulu grinned widely.

Exhausted, Alika sat back, awaiting the arrival of the kayaks. He desperately wanted to step onto land and then go to sleep for a long time.

Alika watched as the kayaks moved steadily toward him, wondering how far away the rescuers lived and how, once ashore, he could find a way to return to Nunatak. That had been on his mind many nights as they drifted.

There had been so many times, especially at night, when he'd thought they'd never survive. He'd never told Sulu about those thoughts and was glad he hadn't. The Little One always deserved hope, and here it was at last.

When the first kayak bumped alongside, Alika asked, "Where am I?"

"Baffin Island," the hunter answered, staring at Alika, Sulu, and Jamka on their piece of ice as if he were seeing strange *tonrar,* sea ghosts. *Apparitions!*

Then he said, "What happened to you?"

Alika said, "It's a long story. I'm from Nunatak."

The hunter frowned. "I hear that's up on Ellesmere."

"Yes."

Alika said, "This is my brother, Sulu."

"What happened?"

"I was sealing six months ago and a berg hit our floe."

"Six months," the hunter gasped. "It's now April and you're still alive?"

The other two hunters were now alongside, listening.

"Please take us ashore," Alika said.

"Of course. My name is Katann. We're from the village of Amadjuak."

"My name is Alika."

Within minutes, Alika slid into Katann's kayak and up into the bow. Sulu was inserted into the second boat, and Jamka crawled up into the third.

Alika fell asleep almost instantly.

There was no way to estimate the number of
hunters who had disappeared in the ice over the past
thousand years. It could have easily happened
to Alika, Sulu, and Jamka.

21

After Sulu shook his shoulder, Alika awakened in Katann's stone-and-sod house, not knowing for a few minutes where he was. Then he remembered what had happened the day before, or was it the day before that? He knew he wasn't home. Jamka wasn't there.

There was a young woman looking over at them. She said, "My name is Uming. You and Sulu have slept a long while. You were asleep when Katann carried you in." Sulu had slept next door.

"My name is Alika. We're from the village of Nunatak, on Ellesmere Island."

"Katann told me," she said.

Alika was dazed, not fully awake.

Uming frowned at him. "Katann said he found you on a piece of ice. That's hard to believe."

"It's true. We were on the ice almost six months. Where is Jamka, please?"

"Outside. I fed him."

"Thank you."

"You and your brother must eat," Uming said.

Sulu said, "I'm very hungry."

"We will help. But first you must eat," said Uming.

It was difficult for Alika to believe that he was safe on land, that the ordeal was finally over, that they had survived. Then he was aware that a small girl was looking at him. He said hello, and she ducked behind her mother's pants.

"This is Meeka," Uming said. "She is two."

Though he couldn't see her face, Alika introduced himself to the child, feeling out of place in this dwelling, not knowing what else to say. He was never good with strangers.

Uming said, "I'll feed you both in a moment." Seal meat was boiling on the *qulliq*.

"We were hunting and a berg knocked the floe away from shore," Alika offered.

"Katann told me," Uming said. "But don't tell me what happened next. Wait until later. Everyone else wants to know as well. We seldom have visitors."

Then Amadjuak wasn't any different from Nunatak, Alika thought. Strangers from the outside were rare, and everyone wanted to hear what they said, every detail.

Uming said, "Katann will be back from hunting soon."

Alika said, "He saved our lives." He went outside, followed by Sulu.

Jamka rose, wagging his tail.

Sulu asked Jamka, "How do you like being onshore?" He knelt down and hugged the dog.

Inside again, Alika didn't realize how hungry he was until he sat down to the steaming meat. Uming also served them caribou stew cooked with blackberry bush, a dish their mama often made.

While they ate, Uming kept asking about Ellesmere Island, about their family.

"Papa's a hunter," Sulu said.

Uming said, "Most men are hunters."

That was true.

"And how old are you, Alika?" Uming asked.

"Fifteen," he replied. He'd had a birthday on the floe.

"You seem much older," she said.

He felt older, much older.

Sulu said, "I'm ten."

At last Katann came through the wooden-framed sealskin door, saying, "Ah, you're both awake."

Alika smiled at him. "Yes."

"How do you feel?" Katann looked younger than Alika's father.

"I'm a little sore and still a little tired. So is Sulu."

"You're a lucky boy," Katann said. "If a gale had hit you, that cake of ice you were on could have turned upside down. The three of you could have died."

"I know," Alika said.

Sulu said, "I got very sick and could have died. I fell into the water. Alika and Jamka got me out."

Katann said, "Let's hope you never have to ride a floe again."

Sulu said, "I never will."

Alika and Sulu soon looked around Amadjuak, a collection of one-room sod-stone-and-sealskin houses, smaller than Nunatak. The barren rocky coastal ground was much the same as in Nunatak, with patches of snow here and there this time of year.

In the late afternoon of the boys' second day in the village, the villagers gathered outside Katann's dwelling to hear Alika tell about the epic voyage of the *Polar Star*. Despite having to stand in the spring cold, they listened raptly to every word.

At supper Alika asked Katann how far he thought they might be from Nunatak.

Katann answered, "How far up Greenland do you think it is?"

"Very far. In the winter, we can walk from Nunatak across the ice to Greenland. I've been told it's fifteen *kabloona* miles over there."

Katann said, "It's only a guess, but I'd say Nunatak is eight hundred white-man miles. You can never make it, summer by kayak or winter by sledge. There are too many bays, inlets, and rivers to cross."

"We'll never see home again," Alika said in despair.

Sulu cried out, "What did you say?"

"But maybe you will see home again," Katann said. "There's an American ship, the *Resolute,* that will be stopping here. It came here last summer on a survey. It is the sister ship to the *Reliance* that was wrecked far up north."

"The *Reliance* was near us!" Alika said. "Trying to reach the North Pole."

"You might talk the captain into taking you along," Katann said.

"I'll try. Oh, I'll try," Alika said.

"Meanwhile, you can help me hunt and fish. You can use Uming's kayak," Katann said.

The next three months went slowly, but Alika stayed busy helping Katann hunt and fish. Sulu went out with Uming almost every day, with Meeka in a pouch on Uming's back, to fish for char, and both Alika and Sulu went out on the summer tundra to help gather food for the winter. It was almost the same as being in Nunatak.

At last, in early July, the expedition ship *Resolute,* looking almost exactly like the *Reliance,* anchored off the village. Alika used Uming's kayak to paddle out, and he tied up at the gangway, hoping to talk to the Inuit dog handlers. He remembered that the *Reliance* had sixty huskies aboard, and he could hear the *Resolute's* dogs howling in their pens.

A white man looked down on him from the main deck, saw them, and disappeared for a few minutes. Then an Inuit dog handler appeared at the top of the gangway and asked Alika what he wanted.

"I need to go to Nunatak with my brother and our dog!" Alika shouted up.

"This is not a passenger ship!" the Inuit shouted back.

"But Nunatak is on your way to the North Pole!" Alika yelled, over the howling dogs.

"You have to ask the captain!" the Inuit shouted down.

"We must go with you!" Alika shouted up. "Nunatak is my home."

"I've never heard of it! Come on up here."

Alika climbed the gangway and said, "Please help us."

The dog handler asked, "Why?"

Alika told him part of what had happened, and the handler relented. "All right, I'll take you to the chief mate. He doesn't understand Inuit. I speak a little English."

"I can help you with your dogs," Alika said.

The middle-aged handler drew in a breath, shook his head saying, "Come with me."

Alika followed him to the chief mate's cabin and listened as the mate and the Inuit talked, the white man glancing at Alika. Finally, the dog handler shrugged.

"My name is Kangio," said the Inuit. "You and your brother can sleep with the dogs. Once we get under way, they'll shut up except before they eat. You also have to work."

Alika followed him back to the gangway.

Alika paddled back to shore as quickly as possible. He couldn't wait to get back to Katann's house to tell Sulu.

"That ship will take us home!" Alika called to his brother.

Sulu shrieked with joy. "When?"

"In a few days."

Sulu jumped up and down and hugged his brother.

Alika said, "You may have to work."

"I don't care. Just so we can go home."

Katann and Uming beamed.

The morning of the day the *Resolute* steamed away, Alika and Sulu went about thanking the villagers, especially Katann and Uming, for all they'd done. Then they boarded the exploration ship with Jamka. It was headed to Greenland to top off its coal bunkers and then would proceed north up the strait.

Alika had never been aboard a ship, aside from the wrecked *Reliance.* He'd never been around talking and laughing *kabloona* sailors, men who seemed to enjoy their work. He'd never felt the amazing power of a steam engine that made a whole ship shake. He'd never gone belowdecks to see burning coal beneath something Kangio called a boiler. He'd never stood at the bow of a ship as the water rushed by, or at the stern, where the water became a churning white trail.

Alika was working with the deck gang, polishing brass and scrubbing the wooden decks until they gleamed. He said to Sulu, "Can you believe all this?"

Sulu replied, "I can't."

Sulu was working in the ship's kitchen, peeling potatoes and washing dishes, pots, and pans. Sulu had never gone aboard the *Reliance*. It had already been dismantled by the time he was born.

On the fifth day of their voyage, feeling the sea wind on his face, Alika decided he would become a sailor, not a hunter.

Sulu said, "I don't blame you."

Alika knew his papa and mama would be disappointed, but it was his life to live. Sailors went around the world, and what a world there was to see, Kangio had said. Alika wanted to go where there was sunlight every day.

He'd go home for a while, hunt for a while, but

sooner or later, he'd find a way to become a sailor, perhaps even on the *Resolute* when it returned from trying to reach the North Pole.

Alika warned Sulu that their papa and mama might not be in Nunatak when they arrived. It was almost August, and all the families would be out on the tundra, hunting, fishing, gathering eggs and plants and all the other food necessities needed for winter. The summer departure from the villages and camps had been happening for centuries, and there was no reason that it would not have occurred this year.

Nor did anyone still in the village know that a ship was approaching, and among its passengers would be Alika, Sulu, and Jamka. They were presumed lost in the strait. Even Maja had given up hope. Miak was the first to see the *Resolute* as it slowly came up to anchor off Nunatak.

Alika, Sulu, and Jamka stood by the gangway, waiting for a boat to be launched to carry them ashore. Sulu said, "I do wish Mama and Papa were here."

"So do I," Alika said. "But we're home, Sulu. That's all that counts. Home again, and we're alive. The sun is up day and night. We'll find Papa and Mama wherever they are."

Standing onshore waving were Inu, Miak, and Sulu's carving mentor, Etukak, just the three of them standing there.

Sulu was holding his carving of Punna to give to Inu. He said, looking over at the dwellings, "Nothing has changed."

"We don't know. We've been gone a long time," Alika said.

Miak had gone back from the shore to the center of the village and was ringing the bell again, again, and again. The chords were as sharp as the points of a hunting lance.

Alika broke into tears and grasped his brother, holding him until they went aboard the ship's boat to take them to the rocky beach. They'd already said good-bye to the *Resolute*'s captain and officers and deck crew, as well as Kangio, who all watched the departure. Even the cook stood near the gangway.

Jamka was at the bow of the boat, front paws resting on the gunwale. He leaped out as the prow ground on the sand. Alika and Sulu, having no possessions, followed him, Sulu kneeling down to put his cheek on the grit.

They both hugged Inu and Etukak. Then they

went on to the meeting hall, where Miak was still ringing the brass bell, and hugged him.

They spent little time inside their empty house. Sulu said, "You see, nothing has changed."

Alika agreed, "Nothing has changed."

They loaded a sealskin bag with dried char and took a walrus intestine filled with freshwater for the early hours of their search. Farther inland, they'd cross many streams and could drink from them. They shed their winter parkas, dressing in their seal-skins, and hurriedly left the house with Jamka.

Sulu said, "You said you think you know where they might be."

"You've been there before. It's the usual village campground this time of year. We'll go northwest and find them," Alika said.

They hadn't walked a mile on the tundra before Sulu said, "It's just like we left it."

Alika laughed. "It never changes on the tundra until the snows come."

The sun was strong, and the fresh air carried the sweet smells of summer. The heather was thick, and the cranberries and blueberries and crowberries were waiting to be picked on the way home.

They walked steadily northwest for two days, stopping only to rest, eat, and sleep a little in the new grass.

In the early afternoon of the third day, they could smell food being cooked far away. Trudging over the top of a low hill, they saw the Nunatak encampment, and it was alert Jamka that first howled and broke into a run for it.

Maja was cooking outside their tent when Jamka practically bowled her over, tugging at her sleeve. She looked up, saw her two sons running toward her, and screamed with joy.

They were home.

Inuit Glossary

aalu	a dipping sauce for meat
aglus	a seal hole (for breathing through ice)
alupajaq	a feast
aqsarniit	people who have died from loss of blood
atertok	a newborn
iglu	a snow house (igloo)
illupiruq	great-grandparents
inua	a heavenly spirit or soul
inuksuk	rock piles (as markers)

Inuktitut	the native language spoken by the Inuit
iynivik	a shelter in which humans give birth
kabloona	a white person
Kokotah	the evil icecap spirit
nanuk	a polar bear
nattiq	a ringed seal
nukilik	to be strong (said of a person)
Nuliajuk	the goddess of the sea
Oqaloraq	the evil snowdrift spirit
piblikoto	craziness
piosuriyok	a brave man
Qilak	a name for the Arctic sky
qulliq	a lamp, stove
Sikrinaktok	a name for the sun
Tatkret	a name for the moon
tonrar	sea ghosts

tornaq	a polar bear spirit
tupilait	the worst evil spirits
tuungait	powerful good spirits
tuvaq	sea ice
ulu	a woman's carved knife
umiak	a large animal-skin hunting boat
unaaq	a harpoon

Author's Note

It was 1942, during World War II, when I came across an account of the most amazing "voyage" in international maritime history: a trip of eighteen hundred miles on a huge ice floe in the Greenland Strait (now known as the Davis Strait).

At the time, I was training to be a third mate aboard the gasoline tanker *Annibal,* sailing both the Atlantic and the Pacific in convoys. Among the books I'd brought aboard was *The American Practical Navigator* (first published in 1802 by the U.S. Navy Hydrographic Office) by Nathaniel Bowditch, a remarkable, complex work including tables for latitudes and longitudes—endless, staggering information that goes far beyond the use of the sextant.

On page 304 was the following: "The best example of a continued drift from the Arctic is that of

Captain Tyson (George E.). On October 14, 1871, he and a party of eighteen others were separated from the polar exploration ship *Polaris,* in latitude 77 or 78 North, just south of Littleton Island, and being unable to regain the ship, remained on the floe."

The nineteen "passengers" on that huge ship of ice survived blizzards, gales, iceberg collisions, encounters with polar bears, starvation, and near mutiny. They included two Inuit men, two Inuit women, and five Inuit children. More than six months after an iceberg tore the floe from its frozen shore anchorage, they were rescued off Labrador. In these times of instant communication, search aircraft, and satellites, it is mind-boggling to consider that they survived six months in temperatures that reached forty degrees below zero. Captain Tyson did not even have a parka.

Fifty-eight years after I'd first read about Captain Tyson, I began extensive research of the astonishing incident. First, I contacted Jane Glazer, widow of David "Pete" Glazer, sports editor of the Portsmouth, Virginia, *Star.* (Pete began teaching me how to write when I was thirteen.) Jane had joined the staff of the Library of Congress, and she arranged for me to copy Captain Tyson's original handwritten manuscript as well as the writings of *Polaris* steward John Herron and crewman Joseph Mauch.

In the end, rather than attempt to boil down the mass of information about Tyson's ordeal—the many characters, the murder of the *Polaris* master, the near mutiny, the shameful treatment of the Inuit—I decided to write a novel about two young boys who were forced to go on a similar journey.

I wish to thank Michelle Konklenberg and Ida Kapakatoak, of the Hunters and Trappers Organization of Kugluktuk, Nunavut, for guiding me to sealing information; John Hickes and Page Burt, of Ranklin Inlet, Nunavut, for information about dog sledges in the 1870s; and author John MacDonald, of Igloolik, Baffin Island, for the lore and legends in his *The Arctic Sky: Inuit Astronomy, Star Lore, and Legend.* MacDonald also suggested Nunatak for the central village of *Ice Drift.* In addition, I consulted *The Inuit Way,* a booklet published by the Inuit Women's Association of Canada; E. C. Pielou's *A Naturalist's Guide to the Arctic*; and Douglas Wilkinson's *Arctic Coast.* Most of the information about ice came from Nathaniel Bowditch's work, but I also relied on I. E. Papanin's *Life on an Ice Floe* (1939) and *Polar Animals* (1962).

While writing Alika and Sulu's adventure, I became so fascinated with the Arctic that I wanted to go to the North Pole. I learned that there are air charters from Nunavut, and pilot Kenn Borek offered to fly me in an Otter, the Arctic workhorse plane. Because of uncertain weather in April or May, I'd be allowed only twenty minutes to stand where Robert Edwin Peary, the man credited with leading the first expedition to reach the North Pole, had stood in 1909. The price for the trip: $87,267.56.

My wallet (and my cardiologist) both nixed the adventure.

Reader Chat Page

1. When Alika and Sulu realize they are stranded on the ice floe, Alika sends the sled dogs home to his parents to alert them that their sons are in trouble. What are other ways that dogs help the Inuit people?

2. What else do Alika and Sulu do to survive? How do they obtain food, water, and shelter? How does Alika know what to do?

3. Alika's father packed the hunting sledge full of items to use in case of an emergency. If you were stranded in the wild, what would you pack in a survival kit?

4. Sulu is more fearful than Alika. What are some examples of Alika's courage in protecting his brother during their adventure?

5. The Arctic may look like a barren place, but Inuit people have thrived there for more than two thousand years. In what ways are Inuit people dependent on nature and their environment?

6. Sulu and Alika were lost in 1868. Can you think of ways that modern technology could have helped lead the brothers to safety?

7. How does this adventure change Alika and Sulu's goals for the future? How does it make them wiser?